I0570488

Finding Home

ATHIS DEY

JENNIFER WRIGHT

Athis Dey
ISBN # 978-1-78430-539-0
©Copyright Jennifer Wright 2015
Cover Art by Posh Gosh ©Copyright March 2015
Interior text design by Claire Siemaszkiewicz
Totally Bound Publishing

Published in 2015 by Totally Bound Publishing, Newland House, The Point, Weaver Road, Lincoln, LN6 3QN, United Kingdom.

Totally Bound Publishing is a subsidiary of Totally Entwined Group Limited.

ATHIS DEY

Dedication

This book is dedicated to my mom. You've not only been supportive throughout my life, but throughout my journey of becoming a writer, and that means the world to me. Your encouragement has given me strength to work through hard times with writer's block, and your love has given me strength to work through life. I love you!

Prologue

Seventy-two years ago

The nursemaid busied herself fluffing the pillows behind her mistress' head, making sure the fragile woman was as comfortable as possible. "There you are now, child. You rest some."

Ryana's delicate hand covered hers. "Thank you, Ragi."

"'Tis my pleasure, my lady." Ragi put on the kindest smile she could, but she knew Ryana could still see the worry in her eyes. Her mistress wasn't faring well and she feared the worst had yet to come. As she ran a cool cloth over Ryana's brow, her gaze shifted toward the woman's swollen belly. If something didn't change soon...

"You are so good to me, Ragi. You always have been." The lady of the house smiled up at her. "I know you'll be just as wonderful with my son."

"Oh, a son you say? And how's it you know that?"

Ryana ran her hand over her abdomen. "I just know."

"Well, I can't wait to meet the young lad, then. I'm sure he'll be just as much of a ball of energy as you were growing up. He'll keep this old woman on her toes yet."

Ryana's soft chuckles sounded in the room, quickly followed by an onslaught of vicious coughs. Ragi quickly grabbed a cup of water and held it to the woman's lips. "Drink, child, and please rest some. You need to save your energy."

Ryana shivered on the bed, and Ragi covered her up further with the blanket.

"Any word of my mate?"

"No, my lady, but I'm sure he'll be back any time now."

Letting out a deep sigh, Ryana closed her eyes. "I honestly don't know what a wizard is going to do to help, but if it makes Vardel happy, then so be it."

Ragi wasn't sure what the wizard could do either, but she had to have faith. With the way Ryana's health was failing more and more by the minute, Ragi would try just about anything to save her mistress. She had been there when Ryana was born, had raised her and been with her ever since. She was now looking forward to helping raise Ryana's child too.

Hours had passed when Vardel finally returned. Ragi suspiciously eyed the man he'd brought back with him, disliking the newcomer immediately. He was an old man with what could only be described as a sinister gleam in his eyes.

Ryana immediately reached out for her mate and Vardel obliged her needs. Rushing to her bedside, he then sat down and took her hand into his. "My dear, I've brought someone to help," he cooed softly.

Shaking her head, Ryana looked past Vardel to the wizard. "I don't know, Vardel. What if something happens to the baby?"

Ragi watched a muscle twitch along her master's jaw. She knew that Vardel had been silently objective toward the baby from the beginning. She'd overheard him talking to others about his dislike of the whole thing. He had the perfect mate who bent to his every whim—a baby would now take her attention away from him.

Ragi had seen all of the looks of disdain and had heard the harsh whispered words. Her master didn't want the child, and if it wasn't for the life of his lovely mate right now, Ragi was sure the man wouldn't have gone so out of his way to help his mate through childbirth.

Vardel reached out and brushed the hairs off Ryana's forehead. "Shh, love, do not worry. The baby will be fine."

Wet streaks covered Ryana's cheeks as she began to cry. "But I love him so much. I don't know what I'd do if anything were to happen to him. Promise me nothing will happen to him...*ever*. Please, promise me you'll take care of him."

Vardel's posture stiffened briefly, but he quickly regained himself and smiled at her. "I promise, love. But you need not worry, because you're going to be just fine."

Ryana's crying set off another bout of coughs. It was a puzzle to them all how it was possible that she was being affected this way. She was a vampire. She shouldn't be having such problems. But somehow, the little child inside her was trying to take her away. Since Ryana had fallen ill, Ragi had witnessed on many occasions her master had gone on rampages, cursing the unborn child countless times—all far away from the ears of Ryana, of course. So Ragi was somewhat shocked to see how easily he now promised such a thing.

Would he live up to it, though?

Ryana whimpered when her coughing ceased, and those whimpers soon turned to cries of pain.

Clutching her stomach, she moaned, "Oh, he's coming. Oh gods!"

Vardel glared at the wizard. "She needs you now. Do something!"

Ragi wanted to protest, but she knew her objections would fall on deaf ears. The only reason Vardel put up with her was because she had been Ryana's nursemaid while the girl grew up, and a dear friend since. Even though Ryana was fully grown and had a mate, she'd still insisted that Ragi stay with her. And, of course, Vardel could never tell his loving mate no.

The wizard hurried over to a nearby table and began removing items from his bag. The odd objects he set out did nothing to soothe Ragi's nerves, but she forced herself to remain the silent servant and do only what she could to ease Ryana's discomfort. While she ran a cool cloth over her mistress' forehead, she watched out of the corner of her eye as the wizard prepared his potion. One thing stood out to her, though she couldn't seem to put her finger on how she knew it or from where. All she knew was that it sent a shiver down her spine. She watched as the wizard delicately handled the beautiful flower—its petals as white as snow, with soft-toned purple blending through them—all the while chanting words under his breath as he broke it into pieces and added it to the potion.

Ryana's cries of pain remained steady, and Ragi was on the verge of speaking up. They had to do something, and this wizard surely could not be the answer. Her chance passed too quickly, though, and before she knew it the wizard was holding the small bowl to Ryana's mouth, insisting that she drink its contents.

Only seconds passed before Ryana's cries settled down. Beyond what everything in her gut was telling her, Ragi felt a small sliver of relief. But the good feeling passed before she could truly enjoy it, because Ryana's sudden gasps had everyone in the room on their feet.

Ragi rushed to the end of the bed and pushed the blanket up. "All right, now, my lady. Slow, deep breaths, child." She had barely positioned Ryana's legs apart when the delivery started—faster than she'd ever seen before. She encouraged Ryana to push but hated hearing the screams of pain her mistress bellowed out.

A lifetime seemed to pass before the sweet cries of the newborn child filled the air. Ragi quickly wrapped the child up and cleaned off as much of the birthing remains as she could.

The baby was beautiful. Holding the newborn up for Ryana to see, she said happily, "You were right, my lady. It's a boy." Her words almost faltered at the sight of her mistress, though. Sweating and very pale, Ryana looked exhausted, but it was the white streaks that ran through her hair that gave Ragi pause. What could have caused such a thing? Not wanting to worry her mistress, Ragi kept her smile steady.

"My boy," Ryana breathed out. "My Khale." She sighed as she sank back further into the bed.

Then she was silent—and the rest of the room fell silent with her.

Vardel slowly leaned in closer to his mate. "Ryana? Love?" He gave the hand he was still holding a gentle pat. "Ryana," he said more sternly. "Ryana!"

It was as if a thousand boulders came crashing down on Ragi, the weight of them stealing her breath away.

Mayhem broke out in the room. The menacing chuckles from the wizard echoed around them, only to be quickly silenced by the blade that was dragged across his throat. Vardel's agonizing and anger-filled shouts sent a shiver down her spine. He continued to cut at the wizard even as the man lay dead on the floor. Her master was going to lose his mind if she didn't do something quickly.

Mustering up her courage to near the lethal man, she spoke softly as she stepped toward him, coming to a stop at his side, "Master, think of your boy. He needs you right now. He—"

Ragi jerked back when Vardel whipped around to face her, his dagger pointed steadily at her. "Get that *thing* away from me!"

Khale began to cry in her arms, and she held him closer as she backed away from her master.

"I want nothing to do with it!" Vardel continued to yell. He charged toward her and Ragi retreated until her back was against the wall. "Do you hear me? Nothing!"

She clutched the baby tighter. "But... But, master, you promised Ryana—"

"Get out!"

The rage that filled her master's eyes had her fleeing the room. She raced through the castle until she was in the safety of her own quarters. Taking a deep breath, she tried to calm the newborn. "Shh, little Khale. Quiet, my boy. Everything will be just fine." Taking a seat in her rocking chair, she sang softly to the baby until his cries faded.

Then the baby looked up to her for the first time and the sight stole her breath away once again. Bright lavender eyes stared back up at her, a pair so lovely and unique that Ragi knew from that moment that Khale was special — a miracle in his own right.

Chapter One

After opening his eyes, Larken blinked several times to clear his vision. Glancing around the room, he knew right away that it wasn't his own. Memories from earlier in the day came flooding back.

Tessa's smooth skin and Corben's calloused hands. Soft touches and fierce kisses. Hard muscles and luscious curves. Her cool breath against his skin. The tight heat of Corben's channel clamped down around his dick as he thrust into him.

He fed from the both of them – the man's blood finally giving him the release his body begged for.

Blinking a few more times, Larken tried to remember what had happened after that, but he couldn't. He must've fallen asleep shortly after, which was a surprise considering that rest rarely came to him these days.

"Well, good evening. Did you sleep well?"

Rolling onto his back, he looked across the room to Tessa, who stood by her wardrobe. Had he slept well? Not really. "Yeah, sure." While stretching his large frame, he moved his arms across the bed and realized something. "Where's Corben?"

Tessa smirked at him. "He left shortly after you fell asleep. You kept trying to push him out of the bed." She let out a soft giggle. "You tried pushing me out, too, but I just pushed back. This is my bed after all. I wasn't about to let you kick me out of it."

Larken chuckled at her remark. Tessa was a tough woman, and he was glad that she had survived the invasion the coven had suffered two weeks prior. Slowly, he sat up and swung his legs over the side of the bed. A chill ran through him from the cold air in the room. The mid December winter was becoming harsh—the temperatures were lower than normal, but at least that kept the snow away. With the long travels he would be taking this evening, though, he'd rather have the snow.

He didn't turn to look at Tessa as she sat down beside him.

"You look a little tired," she commented.

He still couldn't believe he'd actually slept. He considered himself lucky if he even managed to get an hour of rest a day. Every time he closed his eyes, all he dreamed about was *him*. Larken sighed when his chest tightened at just the thought of him. He hated that Zane still got to him the way he did, but Larken was finding ways around it, finding ways to push those thoughts aside—to make himself not care. Granted, others might not think his methods were the best to go with, but he didn't care what anybody else thought.

A delicate hand came up to rest on his shoulder. "Maybe you should sleep some more."

He didn't acknowledge Tessa's suggestion. He was pretty sure it was the feeding that had allowed him to rest so peacefully, and it wasn't as if he had time to do that again. Getting up, Larken walked over to the chair that held his clothes. He remained quiet as he dressed, but was well aware of Tessa getting closer to him.

"You know," she spoke softly behind him, "after all of the years that we've known each other, I like to consider us as friends." She stepped nearer and rested her cheek on his back as she leaned against him, wrapping her arms around his waist. "If you ever want to talk about..." She hesitated when he tensed. "Well, if you ever just want to talk, I'm here to listen."

She came around to stand before him and graced him with a light kiss to his cheek. Looking down at her, he saw the worry in her eyes. He tried to smile, but had a feeling he hadn't been too successful at it.

"I have to go," he finally said.

Tessa rolled her eyes and walked away mumbling, "Stubborn vampire."

Larken truly did smile that time and followed her toward the door. He stopped in the doorway and kissed her cheek as she had done to him. "Thank you."

She waved her hand dismissively. "Yeah, yeah." What playfulness she held faded away. "Take care of yourself, all right?"

He wanted to respond, to assure her that he would, but he couldn't find it in himself to say it.

Would it be lies if I did?

Seeming to understand his hesitation, Tessa just smiled again and gave him a light push out into the hall. "Go on. Get out of here." Brief hatred flared in her eye. "Make sure that traitor burns."

He nodded in agreement then headed off to his room. Tonight he and Keddrick would start their travels to Allengard, where the vampire council was located, and hand Varek over to them to serve him justice for his treachery. The steel box that they'd be transporting him in was sturdy enough to hold Varek at his full strength, but not wanting to take any chances, they'd waited two weeks, weakening the man by barely giving him any blood.

Once Larken reached his room, he went straight to the bathroom to wash off the sweet smell of perfume and dried semen from his partners. He rubbed his eyes as he walked back into his room. He might have gotten sleep, but exhaustion still overwhelmed him. As he stood in front of his wardrobe, the small wooden box on the corner of his desk kept catching his eye. He had told himself that he wasn't going to bring it with him to Allengard, but what he'd taken earlier that day was well out of his system, and the draw of the drug had him slowly inching his way over to his desk. Opening the lid to the box, he eyed its contents. Larken really did need to be in his absolute right mind tonight, but he just felt so...free...when he took it. He needed that. He needed to feel the rush that numbed his emotions. He wanted it. But should he do it?

Pinching the bridge of his nose, Larken closed his eyes in frustration, yet images of Zane flashing through the darkness had him opening them back up again. Nope, he couldn't go without. He needed it. He needed to take it all away.

Larken picked one of the plump licus leaves out of the box and put it in his mouth. He hesitated for a moment, but picturing Zane again had him biting down on the black foliage, its bitter juices flowing over his tongue. After swallowing the rest of the leaf whole, he waited.

It didn't take long for the effects of the drug to kick in. It coursed through his body at an incredible speed. His toes curled against the fur rug beneath his feet as his hands fisted at his sides. Moments passed as his body twitched, trying to fight against the opiate, but he just took in deep breaths and pushed the resistance aside. Finally, he was able to breathe normally again. The buzz humming through him made him smile. He'd never felt more alive, more awake, more uncaring in his whole life than he did when he took the licus.

The little leaves have been the only thing that's gotten me through since…

Larken shook his head. He didn't even want to think about it.

Smiling now at the incredible feeling running through him, he finished getting ready then headed downstairs.

He paced the entry hall as he waited for Varek to be brought up — Keddrick was already outside readying the horses and carriage to transfer their prisoner. He wasn't sure if it was the licus making him feel antsy or if the men truly were taking too long to bring Varek up, but he was ready to go down and get the vampire himself if they didn't hurry up. Crossing the room a few more times, Larken then spun around, ready to head downstairs, but froze in place when he saw Zane standing there.

They could do nothing but stare at each other. He found himself becoming lost in those deep sapphire eyes — eyes that had entranced him so many times in the past. His mind threatened to wander off to moments when they'd been intimate, when they had held each other, when they had devoured each other's mouths in passionate kisses, but he quickly shook the thoughts aside. The empty feeling inside him could not be filled with love from Zane, so he refused to let his mind revel in the pleasures they had once shared.

Zane's mouth opened as if he were ready to speak, but the sounds of the men finally bringing Varek up from the dungeon had him taking a step back.

"Sorry it took so long, sir." Ballen forced the weakened vampire to stand up straighter. "But he actually put up a fight. Best keep a close eye on him."

Larken nodded then gestured for the men to take Varek outside. "I'll be right out."

As Ballen and Corben passed by, Corben looked him over from head to toe—those dark brown eyes seeming to glisten with lust. Larken wasn't sure what was running through the man's head, but whatever it was, Corben had better keep it to himself. Larken had no intensions of 'furthering' their time together. Earlier that day was the second time they'd had sex, but it was just that—sex. He'd have to make sure Corben understood that if they were to ever do it again. Corben was just one of a few that he'd lain with in the last two weeks, and he had no intentions of any of the men or women meaning more to him than a simple release.

Looking back to Zane, Larken caught a familiar expression on Zane's face as he stared at Corben. With the way Zane's eyes were slightly narrowed, it almost seemed as if he disliked the man—a look Larken had found himself giving Bo on more than one occasion.

The hackles on the back of Larken's neck rose at the whole situation. Zane had no right to feel anything about what went on in his life. The man had forfeited that right when he'd chosen a dragon over him.

Their love was lost.

Their friendship perished.

And what little civility that was left between them was slipping away quickly.

Zane didn't love him, and Larken had forced himself to no longer love the man in return — at least, that was what he was trying to do.

Larken was ready to follow his men out of the door when Zane's gaze finally returned to him. Once again they could do nothing but stare at each other. He knew a silent plea was practically bleeding out of the other vampire, but he couldn't find it in himself to respond. Larken could tell that Zane was ready to come closer to him, so Larken took a step farther away.

Zane settled back in his stance. "Be safe," he said quietly.

Slightly tilting his head to the side, Larken assessed him. What was he supposed to say? Was he supposed to care what this man thought?

In the end, the vacant feeling the drug provided him made walking away from Zane so much easier.

Letting out a sarcastic huff, Larken turned on his heels and headed for the door. A steel grip on his heart had him slowing his steps, though, and as much as he tried to fight it, he couldn't stop himself from looking over his shoulder.

He really wished he hadn't. The look on Zane's face further ate at his heart. Most would think the vampire merely looked irritated, but Larken knew Zane better than anyone. The tight line of his lips and the slight downward pull of his eyebrows spoke volumes. He was sad.

Larken felt himself instantly turning around, wanting to comfort him, but he forced himself to stop.

No, he chastised himself. *I don't care for him anymore.*

But then Zane's gaze lifted and met his own, and the hopeful look that filled the vampire's eyes had Larken's chest tightening painfully.

Yes, you do.

It took everything he had, but, with one more glance, Larken forced himself to turn around and this time leave.

He. Could. Not. Care.

Zane's shoulders slumped as the closing of the castle doors shut out the cold evening air. He'd really thought that Larken might actually say something to him this time, but once again he'd gotten nothing. What was it going to take? He knew he'd hurt his friend more than ever, and that he probably deserved everything Larken was—or wasn't—giving him, but he couldn't help but want what they used to have. He knew he was being selfish, but he wanted Larken back, even though he knew how hard it was for the vampire.

Sighing, Zane started toward the stairs but stopped when he spotted Bo peeking his head around the corner. Walking over, Zane smiled to his mate. "Hey."

Bo didn't return the friendly gesture. Instead, his gaze traveled past Zane and to the doors. "It pains him to see us together," he commented.

What happiness he felt at seeing his mate fled with Bo's words. "Yeah, I know." He stood before Bo and cupped his heart-shaped face between his hands. His mate was lovely, and though he would have never normally gone for someone like Bo in the past, he knew that the dragon was meant for him. Bo was his mate, and he loved him more than anything.

"I can't help but wonder if..." Bo pulled his bottom lip between his teeth then released it slowly. "I can't help but wonder if the two of you would have been great together."

Closing his eyes, Zane tried to push away the hurt that sentence caused him. "Stop," he growled. Tightening his hold on his mate, he forced Bo to step closer to him. "Stop questioning us."

"I'm not questioning us," Bo retorted. "I'm questioning the both of you." Bo glanced up at him with fear in his eyes. "There's something between the two of you and—"

"Damn it, Bo. I said stop." He leaned in and nuzzled his mate's cheek, but Bo's hands on his chest pushing him back had him putting space between them.

"I know you love him," his mate whispered.

Zane closed his eyes. There was no winning when Bo set his mind to something. They'd really only been *together* for a little over a week, but he was learning quickly that Bo held onto things longer—and more closely—than he really should. Zane regarded him and hoped that the seriousness he felt was showing. "I do not love him like you think. You're reading into this too much."

Bo frowned at him. "Then tell me no."

It was on the tip of his tongue to reply as the dragon wanted, but he paused. He did love Larken...as a friend. He always would and there was no changing that, but... "It is you my heart belongs to. Why can't you see that?" He brushed his thumbs across his mate's soft skin then placed a tender kiss on his lips. "There will always be a place in my heart for Larken, but it is not the same." Another kiss. "It is you that has my love."

A grin tugged at the corners of Bo's mouth. "I didn't know you could be so sentimental."

"It's a rare showing, so soak it up while you can," he joked back.

Bo's grin slowly faded. "If *we're* it, then why haven't we bonded?"

It was Zane's turn to frown. "What are you talking about? We're already bonded."

Shaking his head, Bo pulled out of his hold. "I am to you, yes, but you have yet to bond to me. Why?"

A twinge twisted in his gut. Having a mate was something he'd stopped dreaming about over a century ago. To have one now, within only a few weeks of meeting the dragon, was haste enough. Why did Bo insist on moving forward even faster? He didn't like feeling crowded. He'd always had the freedom to do as he wanted, to set his own pace, to come and go as he pleased, yet Bo had changed all of that.

Taking a step back, Zane straightened his posture, towering over the small man. In the past, he wouldn't have hesitated to throw back a harsh reply, but this wasn't like before, and this wasn't just anyone. It was his mate. Gritting his teeth, he reminded himself that he had to be gentler than he used to be. Hell, he hadn't really ever been gentle to begin with, but he needed to start if he wanted to keep his mate happy, or if he just wanted to keep his mate period. He *did* want to bond with Bo...someday. He also just couldn't give up on Larken, on their friendship, and he needed Bo to get that.

"I love you, but please don't rush me," he said firmly. "And I want my friendship back with Larken. I hope that you can handle that." Zane silently cursed himself at Bo's hurt look. Groaning, he pulled his mate into his arms and held him tightly. "I'm a selfish old bastard who really doesn't deserve you," he whispered. Kissing the top of Bo's head, he then mumbled into his mate's soft hair, "I told you I was no good for you."

Bo buried his face into his chest. "No, you probably don't. And yeah, you probably are. But, being the idiot that I am, I still love you anyway."

Zane chuckled. "We truly are a twisted pair, aren't we?"

Bo's short laugh was muffled against his shirt as he snuggled in closer to him. It felt good to have his mate in his arms again.

Chapter Two

Gravaick shifted into his human form as soon as his feet touched the ground. With irritation pulsing through his veins, he stormed into the cave. It was beyond pointless now to go out looking for a place to live. Nowhere was there a castle fit enough to house all of his men *and* keep them hidden. He had made the mistake of not setting up another safe haven for them as a backup. He'd put all of his faith into the idea that they'd be living comfy at the coven right now.

"Instead of in this stinkin' cave," he mumbled to himself.

Taking over the coven was supposed to have been a sure thing. How the hell was he supposed to have known that the vampires had a fucking Morvea protecting the place? The mage was an unexpected bump in the road that had basically led to their failure to commandeer the castle. Uvane had managed to escape, but when the man had told him of what he'd seen, Gravaick had just stared at the Drágun in disbelief. *A mover? At the coven?* When the fuck had that happened?

He was aware that Isa was staying with the vampires, but he knew for a fact that she wasn't a Morvea. Besides, Uvane had said that it was a man he'd never seen before. Gravaick had caught wind that the sire had taken on a mate—could his mate be the mage? And when had a Morvea been born? A wizard of that caliber didn't usually go unnoticed. From what Uvane had said, this mage was beyond great. If what Gravaick had been told was true, then this man surely surpassed the stage of simply being a wizard, and instead must hold the title of a warlock. A Morvea warlock was damn near unheard of.

Well, no matter what the case, the mage had thrown a stick into the works. It changed everything. The mover was powerful, so Gravaick knew he'd have to be careful with his future plans of attack.

And there *would* be future plans of attack, because he'd be damned if he was going to stay in this rotting hellhole longer than he had to.

With a little more force than needed, he jerked on his clothes and eyed the incompetent idiots around him. After the battle, he was now down to fifty-three men, and that wouldn't be enough. From what he could tell, the vampires had lost a fair amount of men as well—at least thirty—so he knew they'd have been spending the last two weeks recruiting more men, just as he had been doing.

Gravaick grabbed a drink from a makeshift table and walked over to one of the many small fires. Taking a seat across from Flagos, he glared at the man. If he hadn't needed Flagos' help so much, he'd have murdered him for what he'd done to Nikolai the night of the battle. Gravaick had been so close to getting his Nikolai back, but Flagos had ruined everything. The only small relief he had gotten was seeing that Nikolai had survived the arrow Flagos had embedded into his gut. He was actually surprised that Nikolai had bounced back so quickly after pulling the foreign object out of himself.

"How goes the search to find new men?" he asked Flagos. He'd put the man in charge of finding more Dráguns to replace the ones he'd lost. He knew that not everyone followed his law and joined him when they found out that they were a Drágun. Some men went into hiding to escape serving him.

Stupid, stupid Dráguns. *Do they really think that I don't know about it?* Ha! His people could be so inane sometimes.

"We've gone to almost every village within the dragon countries, and we've only had the two men come forward," Flagos replied.

Tilting his head to the side, Gravaick narrowed his eyes as he studied the man across from him. *Did he say 'come forward'?*

"What exactly is it that you're doing when you visit these villages?" he inquired.

Flagos let out what seemed like a frustrated sigh. "We go to each village, gather everyone to the center of the town, then sift through them and look for Dráguns. Then we advise them that if there are any other Dráguns there, they need to come forward or there will be consequences."

With every word the man spoke, Gravaick's muscles tensed more and more. "You warned them?" he asked incredulously.

Flagos looked at him, seeming to be confused, and nodded his head.

A twitch started beneath Gravaick's right eye as he sat there and contemplated how much he *really* needed Flagos. Could he easily go on without him?

Grinding his teeth, he accepted that he did need the fool. But as soon as he was able to find someone to replace Flagos, he was going to torture the man—slowly.

He still needed an outlet for his rising anger, though.

Unsheathing the dagger hidden in his boot, Gravaick then brought it up and threw it with every ounce of strength he had. Flagos screamed as the blade embedded itself—and a little bit of the hilt—into his right shoulder.

After jumping across the fire, Gravaick pounced on him, pinning him to the ground and clamping his hand down over the Drágun's mouth. "Don't you fucking make a sound," he growled.

Shaking immensely, Flagos whimpered and nodded his head as best he could.

"You warned them, huh? You. *Warned.* Them?" Gravaick pushed down on the Drágun's face, punctuating his last words. "When did we start warning them? I give you one job to do. One job! And you fuck it up." Dear gods, did he really have to do everything himself?

Letting out an exasperated sigh, Gravaick released him and sat back on his heels. Flagos whimpered some more and tears streamed down his cheeks.

"Oh, quit your whining," Gravaick snapped. "You'll heal." Standing up, he dusted off his knees then walked over to the table that held their maps. "I'm taking over the search for more men," he said to no one in particular. They were in need of new warriors more than they were in need of a new place to live.

* * * *

Larken stood by the carriage, trying his hardest not to shiver as his sire spoke to the friendly-looking couple in the doorway of their home. Normally, this trip would have taken them one night, but the cold would make it harder on their horses, so they'd planned it out for two days. By now they should have reached their first stop in Havenbort to rest for the night, but a snowstorm had snuck up on them and had slowed their pace. They were now on the outskirts of Roshend, and the cozy home was the first dwelling they'd come across in over two hours. There were still night hours left to travel, but they didn't dare go any farther in this kind of weather.

He watched with a frown as the male of the household disappeared for a moment, but was happy to see him return with a lantern and a cloak draped around him. The male vampire and his sire quickly jogged over to where he stood.

"They've agreed to let us sleep in the barn," Keddrick shouted over the wind.

"Please, I must insist again," the other vampire spoke loudly as well. "You are more than welcome into our home, sire."

Keddrick shook his head. "We need to stay close to our prisoner, and there is no way I'm letting him into your house. The barn will do just fine."

The man seemed hesitant, but Larken didn't really care where they went as long as they got out of the damn cold.

"Hello, I'm Collin." The vampire stuck his hand out and Larken shook it.

"Larken," he replied in turn.

Collin gestured for them to follow him and he led them to the nearby barn. Larken was more than grateful to get out of the cold. While shaking the snow off his cloak, he looked around the simple structure. A few horses shuffled in their stalls, but otherwise the place was empty of any creatures.

A gust of wind brought their attentions to the door, where a woman hurried in from outside.

"My goodness," she huffed. "I think your food may have gotten cold just from the quick trip here from the house."

"Thank you. I'm sure it's fine," Keddrick assured her as he took the bowls she handed him.

"I do hope you like stew." Smiling, she rubbed her hands together for warmth. "Are you sure you wish to sleep out here?"

"Natty!" Collin scolded. "I already asked him that."

The woman rolled her eyes. "And how was I supposed to know that?"

Larken couldn't help but smile as the old couple bickered back and forth. *It was something me and...*

His smile faded as he refused to finish that thought. His mind did wander, though, to a certain physique, certain deep blue eyes and a body he could roam his hands over for days.

Shaking his head, Larken accepted the stew that Keddrick held out for him.

"Well, if there is anything you need, we'll just be in the house."

"Thank you, Collin. We truly do appreciate your hospitality."

Removing the cloth that covered his bowl, Larken breathed in the hearty aroma from the still steaming contents. While shoveling large spoonfuls into his mouth, he followed his sire over to a small, rickety table. They ate in silence, and he savored the warmth that spread through him from the stew. After eating, they went about making beds out of hay that was piled in the corner of the barn.

"Get some rest," Keddrick rumbled. "We'll leave at nightfall. Hopefully the storm will have passed by then."

Larken nodded as he lay on his makeshift bed and stared up at the roof. He wasn't quite sure if he was in a hurry to continue their trip. This was the first time in a month that he'd been away from Zane—and it was nice. A pressure seemed to have lifted with the distance that was being put between them. He might not actually share a bond with the vampire, but he'd always felt as though there was a connection between them. He had no idea if Zane felt it as well—and now he really didn't care.

It was a relief not feeling it, because as of late, the connection hadn't been too pleasant.

Rolling his eyes, Larken smirked at his ridiculous thoughts. A connection between them? Yeah, right. *It was me. It was all me.* He had created this fantasy in his head of him and Zane, and it was all just that—a fantasy. The connection wasn't real. The love wasn't real. And he really couldn't care less right now.

"Hey."

Larken looked over to the carriage that held Varek.

"Hey, you got anything for me to eat?"

Larken looked over to his sire and found him fast asleep. Looked like the decision was his to make. He wasn't about to bother Collin and wasn't even sure Varek deserved a whole meal, so he got up and went over to their bags, grabbed a chunk of bread, then made his way over to the carriage.

Knowing that Varek was secured by shackles at the front end, he opened the back door without worry of the vampire attacking him.

A sinister smile crept over Varek's face. "I knew you'd still be up."

Larken just stared at him blankly. "Shut up."

He started to reach out to hand the bread over, but stopped when Varek said, "He keeps you awake at night, doesn't he?"

Muscles tensing, he took a step back.

Smiling and nodding, Varek wagged a finger at him. "I knew it." His humor slipped away just as quickly as it had come. The vampire sneered at him. "He keeps me awake too. You see, you're just like me. You hate him as much as I do."

Larken knew of whom Varek spoke, but he refused to play along with the vampire's musings.

"We should have worked together, you and I," Varek said.

Now Larken couldn't keep silent. "I would never do what you did. You betrayed us—your brothers!"

Varek let out a low growl as he stared at Larken. "You all betrayed me first. You let that abomination remain within our home."

"I had no say over Zane staying. That was not my decision to make. And besides, he earned his spot." Larken paused. It had felt like such a long time since he'd stood up for Zane when the other men hassled or talked low of his friend, the action almost seemed foreign to him. Somewhere in the past two weeks, the men of the coven had finally opened their eyes to who Zane truly was. Larken no longer needed to come to the vampire's defense. Everyone seemed to be accepting him now.

It was a triumphant change that he hadn't been able to revel in with the man he'd loved.

It wasn't fair. Varek was right. Zane kept him awake during the day—thoughts of everything they'd had—

and could have had—robbed him of his sleep. Seeing him and the little dragon together...

Zane and Bo were mates, and there was nothing he could do about it.

While chastising himself, Larken placed the bread on the floor of the carriage. He was done thinking of Zane. He was done letting that man rule his thoughts.

Varek reached for the food, but the shackles that bound him had him coming up short.

"Do you mind?" Varek said drolly as he gestured toward the bread.

Smirking, Larken shrugged one shoulder and replied, "Not at all," then closed the carriage door.

He ignored the grumbles from within the holding, and went back to lie down. He knew he would get no sleep, but at least he could rest his weary body for a while.

* * * *

Time seemed to have passed quicker than usual, and before Larken knew it, the sun was setting and Keddrick was rising from his slumber. In silence they went about making sure everything was in order. He could feel Keddrick's stare on him occasionally, but his sire said nothing.

They guided their horses out into the fresh air of the night. Thankfully the storm had passed, and Larken could see the stars. The beauty above him blurred, though, and he blinked through drowsy eyes. Usually, he would fall asleep for at least a few minutes, but not this time. He'd lain awake the entire day, and he was feeling the repercussions. As Keddrick walked away to thank their hosts, Larken quickly pulled the little wooden box from his bag and removed a licus leaf from within. He placed the leaf between his teeth and bit down. It had the same effect as always, and his mind was swimming and alive by the time Keddrick returned.

Keddrick eyed him suspiciously, but said nothing, which he was grateful for, because he'd ingested a slightly larger leaf than normal, and he wasn't sure he could form a coherent sentence at that time. The drug was localized within his head at the moment, and he needed a few more minutes for it to spread throughout his body.

He smiled lazily as his horse automatically began to follow Keddrick's. They reached Havenbort within the hour, and it was only another five hours to Allengard. If they made their stop at Chancellor Vardel's quick, they could be back in Havenbort by the end of the night.

It was no secret that the town was known to have some of the best companions out there — the high prices that were charged said it all. He had plenty of money, though, and maybe he could seek out a little release and warm blood to ease his tired body when they returned.

Yes, the quicker they got to Allengard, the quicker they could get back Havenbort.

* * * *

Handing his cloak over to the butler, Larken then rubbed his hands together in hopes of getting some feeling back to them.

"If you'll follow me, sirs."

He and Keddrick moved in unison behind the old man, who led them to the great room.

"Please, warm yourselves by the fire while I inform my master of your arrival."

"Thank you," Keddrick replied.

Larken took that time to look around the room. Vardel's castle was famous for its size and splendor. The place had to have been bigger than the coven. And for who? Just Vardel and his son?

Shaking his head, he looked over the priceless artifacts, expensive paintings, plush furniture and all the other luxurious items money could buy. *And this is only the great room.*

Was he supposed to be impressed?

"A little over the top, isn't it?" his sire commented.

"You could say that again." He noticed an odd-looking statue on a round table in the middle of the room. Pointing at it, he asked, "What the hell is that?"

Keddrick looked the object over. Shaking his head and shrugging his shoulders, he answered, "I haven't the slightest idea. But I have a feeling it's something valuable."

Snorting at the thought of the ugly thing being worth something, Larken headed over to the fire and tried to get the feeling back in his toes.

It wasn't long before Chancellor Vardel entered the room.

"Gentlemen, how nice to see you." Vardel beamed happily. He gave a slight bow to Keddrick. "Sire, I have been expecting you."

Keddrick kept a steady expression. "Have you?"

"But of course. Word of recent events with the coven has spread quickly." Vardel frowned. "It is a shame that so many men were lost."

Larken tried hard not to show his scrutiny toward Vardel. There was something about the man that didn't settle well with him. Vardel was the picture of any rich man—his posture held firm and tall, his hair was perfectly groomed, smelling strongly of his bath oils, the finest material making up his extravagant clothing, but it was the cane that he held casually that really caught Larken's attention. From what he could see, the staff was made of silver with gold molding that wound up its length, and various jewels were embedded into its intricate artwork. The thing had to have been heavy as hell, which kind of contradicted what it should be used for. Then again, he suspected that Vardel wasn't actually using it to assist him in walking. It was no doubt purely for show. It really was beautiful, though, and Larken guessed that what money had been spent toward it could provide enough food for an entire village for weeks. That in itself stole from its beauty and his appreciation for it.

Tucking the staff between his side and the crook of his elbow, Vardel then clasped his hands together, jarring Larken from his silent judgment. "So, I assume you have brought the traitor? What was his name again?"

"Varek," Keddrick answered. "And yes, he was handed off to your guards as soon as we arrived."

"Well"—Vardel's grin was wide—"I'm glad he's *finally* been brought to us."

Crossing his arms over his chest, his sire stood taller. "As you should know, we had to wait for him to weaken until it was safe to transfer him."

Quickly bowing again, Vardel said, "Yes, of course, sire."

"Well, I assume you and the rest of the council will judge him accordingly. Please send word to me on your ruling. Now, we must be on our way. As you know, there is a lot to be done at the coven."

Larken and Keddrick started toward the door. Larken was more than ready to get out of there and back on the road. Something about this place had him on edge.

"Sire, if I may."

He and Keddrick stopped and turned back at the chancellor's words.

"It would be a great pleasure if you'd stay for a day or so. I'm sure rest is in need."

Keddrick shook his head. "Thank you, but no. Our time is needed elsewhere."

Vardel seemed hesitant, but it was clear that he wanted to say more. Larken had a feeling it was something that neither he nor Keddrick wanted to hear.

"What is it?" his sire questioned.

Steeling his frame, Vardel spoke casually, "The council wishes to meet with you."

Yup, not something they wanted to hear.

"You see, we have some questions that we were hoping you could clear up for us."

Keddrick remained firm with his original answer. "We don't have the time. Just ask them yourself and relay my answers to the council."

"But, sire, I'm sure there are questions that the other chancellors will have that I don't know of. They truly do wish to meet with you. It won't take up too much of your time—maybe a couple of days."

"Why so long?"

"Since no one knew when you'd show up, their regular plans held, therefore some are away at this time."

His sire remained silent for a moment. Releasing a deep breath, Keddrick finally said, "Fine. Send word for their immediate return. We will meet tomorrow evening and then we'll be on our way. Those who can't make it will just have to meet with me at another time."

Vardel grinned and bowed his head. "Thank you, sire. I will send the word out right away." He motioned for one of his servants. "Show them to a guest suite."

"Yes, sir."

"Larence here will show you to your quarters and will gather you for dinner. If there is anything you need just ask him."

"Thank you," Keddrick replied drolly.

His sire clearly wasn't happy to be staying the night, and neither was he. *So much for finding a companion in Havenbort.*

* * * *

They were ushered down for dinner hours later, and it was then that Larken got to meet Vardel's son, Khale. The vampire was quite a sight. Larken knew that Khale was seventy-two years old, but the man was still so young in his eyes. Age aside, it was hard not to stare. Larken could only imagine the firm muscles making up the lean frame that was hidden under Khale's clothes, and his fingers tingled in hopes of gliding over them. The young man was handsome—more so than any other vampire he'd seen. He was unique, to say the least, with his incredibly long hair. It wasn't its length, though, that held Larken's attention. It was that fact that it was white with streaks of lavender running through it. He had known that Khale would look like this. He'd been told the story of how Khale was born and what had happened to his mother. Still, Larken had never seen anyone like him before, and it was hard not to stare slack-jawed when he was introduced to the vampire. To everyone else the boy was normal, but to Larken, he was captivating.

And that accent. The sound of his voice, the way his words practically flowed like music from his lips... It was astonishing. He'd only met with a few others from here before, but none of them had as strong an accent as Khale did—not even the boy's father.

I wonder who he gets it from?

Larken frowned at his thought. He didn't care where Khale got it from. He just wanted to hear it humming around his dick.

Larken spent almost the entire dinner looking at Khale. He couldn't seem to *not* look. He was intrigued and fascinated—not to mention his body was taking a certain interest as well. He watched as Khale carefully wiped the corners of his mouth with a linen napkin. Seeing those plump lips move beneath the man's touch had Larken's cock twitching with need. He pictured those lips tight around his dick, Khale's slick tongue sliding along the underside of his cock, his cheeks hollowing as he sucked him.

The ending of dinner pulled him from his thoughts. Larken stood with the others then exited the dining hall with Keddrick. His sire headed toward the stairs that would lead them to their guest room, but Larken held back. Seeming to notice that he wasn't following, Keddrick turned back to him.

Clasping his hands behind his back, Larken stood there with ease. "You know, I'm not all that tired, I think I'll just wander around for a bit. My legs still need some stretching from our travels." Well, it was partly true.

Keddrick just arched an eyebrow and regarded him. "All right, but please try to get some rest today, I need you at your fullest attention tomorrow."

Larken nodded. "Of course." He wasn't looking forward to meeting with the council any more than Keddrick was—both of them expressing that the council was surely about to stick their noses where they didn't belong. He was, however, looking forward to the possibilities of today's events. Watching Khale walk away just then had his feet itching to follow.

He casually started down a hall opposite to the direction Khale had gone, but as soon as his sire disappeared up the stairs, he switched directions. He'd noted a certain musky scent coming from Khale earlier, no doubt from the richest bathing oils one could buy, but it was deep and dark, not the usual sweetness a lot of bathing oils tended to have. It enthralled him, and he followed it now down the eastern corridor then up two flights of stairs.

Poking his head around the corner, he spotted Khale halfway down the hall about to enter a room. Resuming a casual posture, Larken strolled out into the open and headed Khale's way. Just as Larken wanted, Khale stopped and turned toward him. As Larken grew nearer, he let his powerful stature show, and it had the effect on Khale that he was looking for. Khale seemed to fidget slightly the closer he got. By the time Larken stopped before him, he could see that the man's breathing had increased.

Larken smiled. This vampire was his for the taking.

Chapter Three

Khale narrowed his eyes at Larken as a smile spread across the vampire's features. "Is there something you need?" he asked sharply. "Shall I summon a servant?"

Larken's eyes slowly raked over him, his stare making Khale slightly uncomfortable.

"No," Larken replied, the small grin still tugging at the corners of his mouth. "I think I've found just what I'm looking for."

Khale's body warmed under Larken's accession, but the cockiness in the man's tone had him going rigid. He wanted to scoff at the implication of Larken's comment. Khale wasn't stupid. Through his peripheral vision he'd watched the man staring at him with hunger in his eyes all throughout their meal. Who did Larken think he was? *Who the hell does he think I am if he thinks he can have me so easily?* The man was nothing but a warrior, whereas Khale was a high member of society.

Logically, he could ridicule the man all he wanted, but his body had its own demands. The moment he saw Larken outside the dining hall, something sparked to life inside him, something he had forced away for so many years — his attraction for other men.

"No son of mine will ever be a sodomite!" his father had screamed over and over when he'd caught Khale with Emel, one of the male servants. Khale had been forty then. He and Emel had been together in secret for almost fifteen years. They hadn't been in love, but they did care for each other and enjoyed each other's company. Yet he hadn't been able to do anything when his father had Emel sent away. The man had actually had *all* the male servants replaced with women. Wanting nothing more than to please his father, Khale had given up. Over the years, Khale had suppressed his urges and his father had slowly reintroduced male servants with Khale's promise that it would never happen again.

It had now been thirty-two years since he'd been with another man. It was easy to push his desires to the back of his mind, because none of the other men in his life even caused his dick to twitch. They were all like his father — or wanted to be like his father. No matter the age, they all tried to appease Vardel in every way.

Khale had been surrounded by men that held no appeal for him — until now.

Apparently he was taking too long to reply, and Larken's grin slowly faded until he held a careless expression. Shrugging his shoulders as if his proposal was of no care to him either way, the warrior turned and headed back the way he'd come.

Khale's heart sped up as he watched Larken walk away. He couldn't do this. He *shouldn't* do this. He had done just fine finding his release with countless women, burying his desires for men long ago. He'd gone this long, he didn't need it now.

"Wait." Khale sucked in a sharp breath as the word left his mouth. He watched in horror as the warrior turned around to face him, that cocky grin back in place. He began to tremble as Larken neared him, but refused to let the man see it. With his chin lifted, Khale kept a steady expression as Larken stopped before him, closer than he had the first time. He could feel the heat radiating off the warrior, and it excited him even more.

A niggling in the back of his mind scolded him for his thoughts, but Khale ignored them. Later on that evening the warrior would be on his way after the meeting with the council, and Khale would never have to see him again — well, at least probably not for a *really* long time. So what harm could come from him fulfilling his desires for one day? His father would never know.

Without saying a word, he reached out and pushed the door to his quarters open farther. The warrior's eyes gleamed as he lifted his chin and gestured for Khale to enter first.

Khale kept a stiff posture as he entered his living room, his stomach twisting with anticipation and fear when he heard the door close behind him. He watched as Larken slowly wandered around the room, popping his head into every doorway he came across.

Larken let out a low whistle as he finished his trek. "Living well, I see."

"I suppose," he replied firmly. "From what I hear, the quarters at the coven are plenty suitable."

Larken stopped and gave him a flat look. Khale wasn't sure what he'd said to cause such a reaction, but he didn't really wish to discuss their living arrangements anyway.

Tilting his head to the side, he sighed as if he were bored. He couldn't let the warrior see how much he wanted this.

That cocky grin returned as Larken started his way. Khale didn't move an inch as the man assessed him once again, circling around him then coming to a stop behind him. His breath hitched when Larken touched the loose hairs at the back of his neck. The warrior's fingers then brushed against his back as he wrapped his hand around Khale's braid then followed its length down to the curve of his ass. A tingle ran along his spine as Larken's touch lingered there, his ass clenching with anticipation at how close that hand was to his entrance.

But every erotic feeling fled when he felt the tug at the end of his braid. Spinning around, he slapped Larken's hand away. His nerves grated as the man chuckled and held his hands up in surrender—the tie to Khale's hair held between his fingers.

Glaring at him, Khale snatched the tie back. Pulling his braid over his shoulder, he quickly made work of re-braiding what hair had come loose then tied it off with the leather cord.

"All right," Larken said on another chuckle. "The hair's off limits. Got it."

Khale wanted to snap back at him, but the hungry look that quickly filled the warrior's eyes had his body once again coming to life.

What was it about Larken that did this to him?

He froze in place as Larken leaned in closer to him, his breathing becoming ragged as he watched Larken's tongue slowly glide along his bottom lip. He hated that this man had such an effect on him, but he yielded willingly when the warrior cupped his face within his large hands. His heart raced as Larken's breath ghosted across his lips. Unable to wait a moment longer, Khale closed what little distance there was left between them and crushed their mouths together.

Khale moaned as Larken pressed their bodies together. He wasn't usually one to be dominated, but he had no problem letting Larken take the lead. That notion should've bothered him, but his painful erection took precedence over his thoughts.

Larken's tongue slipped into his mouth and Khale shivered with desire. With a firm hold on his face, the warrior walked backward toward his bedroom, both of them ravishing each other's mouths as they stumbled along. Once there, Khale finally gave in to temptation and touched Larken. Larken's muscles tensed beneath his hands, the hard feel exciting Khale even more. He could picture Larken above him, taking him in every way.

He wanted it.

As if sensing his thoughts, Larken broke the kiss and stared down at him. "Get undressed," he growled out.

Shaking with need, Khale removed his clothing, his gaze never leaving Larken as the warrior stripped as well. The man was stunning. Every inch of him was perfectly sculpted. He was built and hard and made for Khale's touch.

Khale reached out, wanting to run his fingers along the rippled abdomen, but instead gasped when Larken pushed him down onto the bed. No one had *ever* dared do such a thing to him. No one would ever think of pushing him around. With his mouth open, ready to protest what Larken had done, his words failed him. Larken covered his body with his own, the warmth of his skin seeping into him, making his dick grow harder than he thought possible.

Larken glared at him as he took hold of Khale's wrists and held them above his head. "Don't move."

Khale wanted to protest again yet found himself nodding in compliance. The feel of Larken's lips trailing along his throat made him tremble even more. When the warrior nipped at the crook of his neck, Khale couldn't stop the whimper from escaping him. Arching his hips up, he rubbed his hard length along the curve of Larken's hip, moaning again at the sweet pressure it provided.

To his dismay, Larken lifted himself up, severing the touch between them. "I said *don't move*."

With his chest heaving with every breath he took, Khale quickly nodded his head again.

Larken smiled at him—that cocky grin that Khale was quickly starting to hate—but his irritation faded as Larken took hold of his cock. Groaning, Khale bucked his hips, wanting so bad for that hand to stroke him.

A sparkle shone in Larken's eyes and the man tightened his grip.

Khale's needy trembles were clearly showing now. It was cruel how the warrior was torturing him with teasing touches, but he had a feeling he knew what Larken was waiting for, and there was no way he was going to say it.

Larken squeezed his dick again.

"Please," he begged. Khale immediately cursed himself. How could he have let the word slip from his mouth so easily?

Lust filled Larken's eyes and he slowly moved his hand up and down once. Khale groaned and bucked his hips again, needing for him to move faster, but Larken just stopped completely.

Oh, to hell with this no moving shit. It'd been too long for him to lie around and play games. Not wanting to be the yielding bottom anymore, Khale wrapped his hand around Larken's and forced the man to stroke his cock. "Oh gods!"

Suddenly, Larken's body was on him again, their mouths locked firmly together. Khale ignored the wanton noises he was feeding Larken and instead relished the moment. It'd been so long, and he was now so close.

Within the blink of an eye, his hands were once again above his head. Still not wanting to yield, he wrapped his legs around Larken's waist and arched his hips, grinding against the curve of the man's hip again.

Larken growled into his mouth. Releasing his wrists, Larken wound an arm around him and pulled Khale farther up onto the bed so Khale could rest his head on the pillows.

Khale threaded his fingers through Larken's hair as he plundered his mouth, and the warrior began to grind his own erection against him. He gasped again, this time when he was met with the cold air in the room. His surprise quickly subsided when Larken flipped him over onto his stomach almost effortlessly. He was a little taken aback by the power Larken used on him. It wasn't like he was a small man by any means. Sure, Larken was a little more built than him, but he felt almost feeble as the man seemed to toss him around like it was nothing.

Larken's hard body covered his and once again Khale found himself at a loss for words. The warrior forced his legs apart as he settled between them, his hard length firmly pressed against Khale's ass.

"I'm tired of waiting," Larken growled into his ear.

Unable to speak, Khale lifted his head from the pillow and nodded. Larken grabbed Khale's hands and held them above his head, making Khale feel so open and exposed. Taking hold of both wrists in one of his hands, Larken then touched the fingers of his free hand to Khale's mouth and Khale gladly accepted them, sucking on them until they were wet.

Larken reached between them, his wet digits pressing against Khale's entrance. Khale shuddered as a finger circled around his hole, the air in his lungs leaving him in a rush as Larken pushed one in as deep as it would go.

"Sweet gods, you're so tight," Larken breathed out. He wasted no time adding a second digit then a third.

Khale could do nothing but writhe beneath him as Larken fucked him with his fingers.

"Where's the oil?"

Khale heard the question, but couldn't speak past the moans that escaped him.

"The oil," Larken said more forcefully as he pulled his fingers out of his ass.

Khale cringed at the sudden loss but finally found his words. "Th-the bedside table. In the drawer."

Thankfully, Larken wasted no time in finding the bottle and lathering himself up. The man's slippery fingers circled his hole again, and Khale was ready to push back and impale himself on them, but the head of Larken's dick there had him freezing. Grabbing Khale's hips, Larken held him in place as he pushed inside.

Khale gritted his teeth against the abrupt fullness — his channel stretching as Larken filled him to the hilt. It was *that* feeling that reminded him of how much he had missed this.

Larken pulled out then thrust back into him and Khale braced his hands against the headboard to keep himself in place. A euphoric sensation consumed him, and he buried his face into his pillow, crying out over and over again at the feeling.

When Larken wound his arm around him and pulled him up, Khale just did as instructed. Larken nudged them forward until they were on their knees and Khale's dick was pressed against the headboard.

Taking hold of Khale's hands, Larken placed them over the top of the headboard and said, "Hold on."

Sweat rolled down Khale's back as he took everything the warrior gave him. Larken pounded into him with an unrelenting force, and Khale loved it. He'd never felt more alive than he did right then.

Looking over his shoulder, a surge of desire flooded him as he took in the pleasure etched on Larken's face—his eyes squeezed shut, his mouth open as he panted for air, his forehead creasing as his brow pulled down in a painful-pleasured look.

Dear gods, the man was beautiful.

The heat around Larken's dick had his head spinning. Even with his eyes closed, he could see it all. *That hard ass there for the plucking. That long cock that's mine to tease. The broadness of his shoulders. The firm abs that lead to a narrow waist.*

Larken increased his pace, his hips plowing forward with everything he had, his mind reeling as the visions filled his head. *His square jaw, thin lips, narrow nose...*

And those beautiful sapphire eyes.

No! Remember who you're with. Do not think of Zane.

When he sensed a gaze on him, Larken opened his eyes and his movements faltered at the pale lavender orbs that stared back at him. Aside from the sudden guilt about what he'd been thinking, a feeling sparked inside him—one that he really didn't want to try to decipher right then—so he grabbed Khale's chin and forced the man to look forward again. He couldn't look at him—not now. All he wanted to do was bask in the pleasure he was feeling. The man was so tight, and he'd nearly lost his mind when that snug channel had enveloped his cock.

Leaning his head down, he latched his lips onto the curve of Khale's neck and sucked hard. He held on tightly to Khale as the vampire shuddered within his arms as he came. Larken longed to bite him, to pierce his skin and take what he wanted, but he held back.

Once Khale's tremors calmed, Larken brought his hands up and over Khale's chest and clamped onto his shoulders. Using the leverage, Larken pulled Khale down onto his dick every time he thrust up. Khale rested his head on Larken's shoulder as he arched his back, allowing Larken to slip in deeper.

Larken couldn't stop the roar that escaped him as his orgasm ripped through him, and he continued to thrust relentlessly as Khale milked every last drop of cum from his cock.

Finally sated, he let the both of them fall backward onto the bed, exhaustion quickly overtaking him. Rolling onto his side, he then snuggled down into the disheveled blanket beneath him and let out a soft, pleasurable sigh when a hand came to rest on his hip. His breathing evened out as fingertips lightly traveled back and forth across his skin, soothing him. He hadn't been this relaxed in... He didn't know how long. Warmth settled over him, and for once he could let himself go, could rest peacefully.

He'd almost drifted off to sleep when he felt the heat of someone's gaze on him again. His breath caught when he peeked through his eyelids and saw Khale lying there staring at him.

A flutter spread through his stomach, catching him off guard. The sensations that vibrated through him when looking into Khale's eyes comforted him, and he didn't like it.

It scared him.

Mentally shaking his head at the ridiculous thought, he sat up then swung his legs over the side of the bed. He had to get out of there.

Larken scrubbed his hands over his face then stood up and walked over to where his clothes lay scattered across the floor. He heard movement from Khale, but didn't look at him. It wasn't until he noticed the vampire's footsteps getting farther away that he finally glanced up. Khale had donned a plush, fancy-looking robe and was currently making his way to what Larken assumed was a bathroom.

Stopping in the doorway, Khale glanced back at him. "I'm sure you know your way out."

Larken couldn't help but grin. *The little shit is trying to show his authority now? Like hell.* "Oh, trust me. I was already heading that way."

Khale failed to hide his shock, and that just made Larken chuckle. *Yes, the lowly warrior fucked you – the aristocrat. Deal with it.*

Larken held the vampire's gaze as he slipped on the last of his clothes. Khale just stood there, his mouth still agape as Larken headed toward the door. "'Twas a pleasure, my lord," Larken said sarcastically as he walked backwards out of the room, saluting Khale as he went.

His smile remained as he left the living quarters. Having to face Khale again later that evening was going to be fun, because he had a feeling that their parting just then would be all Khale could think about at the meeting.

For some reason that pleased him, knowing that he'd got the best of him in the end. *You think you have authority over me? Think again.*

As Larken left Khale's quarters, a slight sense of regret filled him — not for having had sex with Khale, but for the way he'd acted. Picturing Khale in his mind, Larken focused on the look of surprise on the man's face, and he felt the sudden urge to go back and kiss the expression away — only wanting to see a smiling Khale instead.

Shaking his head, Larken pushed silly feeling aside. Khale had treated him just as childishly, which Larken figured was something Khale usually did with his lovers. Why should he worry about how he had acted?

* * * *

Pulling the thick fur blanket up over his chest more, Khale tried to get some sleep. His mind wouldn't stop reeling at what he'd done. He'd let another man into his bed. He had given himself over in the most intimate way to someone he barely knew. It frightened him a little. What was it about the warrior that had him letting down his guard and all sense of rationality? What had possessed him to act such a way? He was in absolute disbelief that he'd permitted such a thing to happen. He knew better.

But it wasn't just the shock of what he'd allowed himself to do that robbed him of his sleep, it was the visions of Larken's departure and the words the warrior had so brashly said that refused to give him peace. Being dismissed so quickly had stung, and Khale would admit that he hadn't reacted in the best way. What he'd said to Larken first had been just as demeaning and rude. But seeing Larken getting dressed, knowing that what they'd shared meant nothing more than a quick release, had hurt him, so he'd lashed out.

Good gods, maybe his father was actually wearing off on him.

Khale shuddered at that thought. He loved his father, and wanted nothing more than to please him, but he had no desire to *be* his father.

Sighing, Khale relaxed his body and mind and drifted off into a deep sleep.

The warrior is on his knees before him, staring up at him with love and lust in his eyes. Larken wraps his arms around Khale's waist and rests his head against his stomach. Khale idly runs his fingers through Larken's hair, enjoying the closeness they're sharing. They make love – a joining that is far sweeter and softer than he's ever experienced. Feeling Larken pulse inside him, he teeters on the edge of his own orgasm...

Khale yelped as he was yanked from his bed, his arms flailing as he hit the ground. On instinct, he curled into a ball and waited for what was sure to come. What always came. And he wasn't disappointed.

He gasped as pain sliced through his ribcage.

"How dare you!" his father yelled as he brought his cane down on Khale's back again. "How dare you betray me!"

"But I haven't, Father," Khale whimpered as best as he could.

"Haven't you, though? You think defiling yourself by letting another man into your bed isn't a betrayal to me? You promised me, Khale!" His father's breathing became ragged as the man beat him.

Khale cried out when one of his ribs cracked. "Please, stop! I haven't—"

Vardel crouched over him and grabbed him by his chin, forcing Khale to meet his fiery gaze. "You dare lie to me now?" He smacked Khale across the face, hard. "You were seen letting Larken into your room, where he stayed for quite some time." He slapped Khale a second time. "Did you think I wouldn't find out?" Vardel continued to beat him with his cane.

"I'm s-sorry, Father," he stuttered, praying that the pain would soon end. He should have known that his father would find out. He wanted to curse Larken for getting to him the way he had. He'd managed to go so long without. How could he have been so stupid as to give in to his desires?

"What am I going to do?" Vardel asked on a rush of air. He paused with his cane raised above his head. "I have important plans in the making, Khale, and unfortunately you play a big part of it. How am I to trust you, though?"

Plans? He didn't know of any plans. But it wasn't as if his father usually included him in any of his business. Vardel saw Khale as one thing only— another one of his servants—more or less.

Vardel took hold of Khale's chin again. "I need to know," he growled out. "Are you with me or not?"

All Khale had ever wanted was for his father to love him, to even at least acknowledge him as his son. "Yes," he croaked. "Yes, Father, I am with you. Always."

Vardel sneered and roughly pushed Khale's face into the floor. "Good. Now, I want you to remember *this* next time you think about letting another man into your bed."

Khale sucked in a sharp breath when his father's cane connected with his genitals.

Gasping for air, he lay bleeding and broken as Vardel walked away. He choked on the sobs that tried to escape him. So many times he'd endured lashings and beatings from his father, but nothing as bad as this.

Not even bothering to try to make his way to the bathroom to clean up, Khale remained on the floor, praying for the pain to ease. He had done this to himself. This was all his fault. He had let himself feel things he shouldn't, and now he was paying for it.

Shaking uncontrollably, he stared up at the ceiling and let his mind drift — drift to another time, another life, where his mother was with him and his father loved him. It was a fantasy that had gotten him through this before, and he needed it now more than ever.

He hadn't realized he'd fallen asleep again until a sudden gasp awoke him.

"Oh my sweet gods!"

Khale slowly blinked his eyes open.

"Oh, child. Oh, how could he do this?"

Swallowing to wet his dry throat, he said roughly, "Ragi, don't."

"Don't you go ordering me around now, boy," Ragi tsked as she knelt down next to him. "He has gone too far this time. I could murder that man right now," she grumbled to herself.

"Un-uh." Shaking his head, he took her offered hand. "Please, don't. He just—"

"I swear, boy, I'll beat you myself if you even think about defending him to me."

"Ragi, please."

His nursemaid's eyes narrowed at him. He could see her anger and the love for him burning in her gaze and he adored her for it, but if she tried to confront his father, it would only make things worse.

He stared at her, silently begging.

On a huff, she looked away. "Now, you very well know I can't deny you when you look at me like that."

He was surprised to feel himself actually smile. He leaned over and kissed her cheek. "Thank you, Ragi."

Trying to hide her blush, she shook her head. "Don't thank me yet. I still might poison his food—for fun, of course."

"Of course."

Tsking again and rolling her eyes, she then proceeded to help him to the bathroom. Ragi gasped when she stood behind him—no doubt in shock at the sight of his back. "Oh, Khale," she breathed out.

He could only imagine what his back looked like, but he needed to reassure her that he'd be all right. "It's fine. It probably looks worse than it really is."

"Even here?" she asked as she gently touched his side.

Khale's stomach plummeted and his knees nearly gave out from the pain. Gripping the counter until his knuckles turned white, Khale tried not to throw up.

"As I suspected. You have a broken rib." She tsked again as she poured some water into a basin.

"You know," he gritted out, "that sucking noise between your teeth is more painful to my ears than anything else."

"Very funny, young man." She lightly ran a wet cloth over his back. "I don't know how he can do this to you," she said quietly. "He knows you have a harder time healing."

Khale stared at his reflection as his nursemaid tended to him. His skin was paler than normal, his eyes a shade darker than their usual vibrant color. Ragi was right. It would take twice as long for him to heal as it would any other vampire. "I think that's why he does it," he mumbled to himself. Ragi had told him long ago that it was an unfortunate trait that his mother had as well. He had questioned whether he was a half-breed, but she had assured him that he was as much of a pureblood as they got. No one could figure out why his mother had held such an anomaly, and it was no different for him. He just had to be more careful.

"Maybe you should skip the gathering," she suggested.

"No." He looked back at her in the mirror. "Father expects me to be there." And apparently the man had plans for him, and Khale guessed that it was at this gathering of the council that those plans would be made known. If what his father had said before was true, then he *had* to be there when they were revealed. "Just love me as I know you do, and be the doting nursemaid and help me get dressed. I don't think I can quite do it myself right now." He smiled at the frustrated sigh she gave him as he walked—hobbled was more like it—back into his bedroom. "The midnight blue dress coat, if you please." It took some time, he moved slow and gingerly, but they finally managed to get him dressed.

As part of her usual routine, Ragi came to his room every evening, making sure he was up and ready to start a new day. Khale liked to think that was why his father beat him at such times during the afternoon, because Vardel then knew that Ragi would be there to help Khale later, and Khale couldn't let himself think otherwise. He needed to hold onto some hope that deep down his father loved him.

Chapter Four

Larken tried not to make a sour expression as he walked with his sire into the gathering room. The licus he'd just ingested was leaving a more unpleasant taste in his mouth than usual.

He looked around the room, observing the two rows of chairs that lined the walls to his left and right. They were impressive pieces, with high backs and plush cushioning—six of them in each row. There was also a smaller, plain-looking chair that sat by itself at the end in between the rows. Then at the head of the room, upon a raised platform covered by a fur rug, sat the biggest chair—its wood thicker, jewels embedded into its frame, its cushions a royal red instead of black like the others. It was as if it was meant to completely stand out from the others—and it did.

No doubt the tiny chair was an added piece for Keddrick, and the grand chair was Vardel's. But from the sideways glance and an arched eyebrow his sire gave him, he knew that Keddrick would have none of that. Striding through the hall as if he owned the place, Keddrick took his seat in the masterpiece that towered over the others with Larken standing at his side.

The council members slowly trickled in as an hour passed. Like Keddrick, Larken was growing impatient. He was ready to get the hell out of this place.

As Larken glanced around the room, he leaned closer to Keddrick. "You've got to love their accents."

Lowering his voice so that just Larken could hear him, Keddrick said, "In the Earth realm, their accent would be known as a European accent. It's quite strange, though, as it seems to be a mix of multiple places — the United Kingdom, France, Russia, Bulgaria and even Spain. Yet, unlike Earth, their vocabulary is still like ours. I think you'd get a kick out of hearing a true Scotsman speak. Your mind would be completely boggled in the end, but you'd be hypnotized all the same."

Larken regarded everyone in the room. "They sound so prim and proper."

Keddrick gave him a sideways glance. "They are prim and proper."

Making a face of detachment, Larken stood up straight again. "Oh, yeah. Damn."

Keddrick snorted then quickly schooled his features as someone neared them. "Chancellor Vivins," he kindly greeted the lovely woman who was the last to join them. She was the only one to actually approach them so closely, her arms going round Keddrick's shoulders in a brief hug. "How nice it is to see you again."

She smiled and bowed to him. "As always, sire, it warms my heart to have you here. It has been too long since you've last visited."

He returned her friendly smile. "Things have been busy."

Her grin slipped from her features. "Yes, I supposed they are." She glanced over to him and Larken stood up straighter under her gaze. "Ah, you must be Larken."

He slightly bowed his head. "Chancellor Vivins. It is a pleasure to meet you."

Her gaze softened as she got closer to him. "Congratulation on becoming Second Commander. I can tell the position will suit you well."

Larken's gut twisted a little at her words. "With all due respect, Chancellor, I do not believe in which way I gained this title warrants congratulation."

Once again, her sweet smile fled. "I suppose not. But, all the same, I feel you're a good fit and will do great things."

The twinge in his chest caught him off guard. He wanted to do right by Aliam. The man had made him promise to do better than he had, and Larken planned on keeping that promise. "Thank you, Chancellor."

She lightly patted his arm then turned and took her seat among the others. Larken felt his sire's gaze boring into the side of his head. He glanced at Keddrick out of the corner of his eye. Swallowing hard, Larken quickly stared straight ahead again.

"Next time," Keddrick whispered, "just shut the fuck up and say 'thank you'."

"Yes, sire." Larken wanted to kick himself in the ass for that one. What in the hell had made him open his mouth and talk negatively to a council member that he was meeting for the first time? Sure, he'd seen all of them from afar before, but had never had the opportunity to work directly with them. He needed to start acting in a manner that befitted the position that he had been respectfully given.

Damn licus. It was messing with his head more than usual.

At that moment Vardel entered the gathering room, his gaze immediately going to Keddrick then flickering to the chair Keddrick was sitting in. Larken gave his sire credit for not smirking at the man.

Vardel said his greetings as he made his way to the front of the room. His stiff posture covered in the fine and elegant materials had him standing out among the others. The man had no problem displaying his wealth, and the arrogance of it grated on Larken's nerves. Vardel thought himself better than everyone else, and the man didn't bother to hide it.

"Sire," Vardel said with a bow. "I thank you again for taking your time to hear our concerns."

"Concerns?" Keddrick arched an eyebrow as he stared down the chancellor. "Last night you said you and the others had questions—not concerns."

Vardel splayed his hands and shrugged his shoulders. "A miscommunication. My apologies."

Miscommunication my ass.

Keddrick clearly seemed perturbed by the disregard in Vardel's voice, but there was nothing that could be done about it now. "Fine. Let's get on with it then," his sire ordered.

The chancellor's smile never faded as he turned around to face the others. "Thank you, everyone, for coming on such short notice. If you'll please be seated, we'll begin."

After the few wandering about had found their seats, Vardel proceeded to slowly walk up and down the room with his hands clasped together. "I'm sure you'll all agree with me that there have been some unfortunate events that have fallen upon the coven as of late." The people around the room nodded almost in unison. At the far end of the room, Vardel turned to face them. "Sire, I mean no disrespect when I say this, because as you can see we're all very concerned, but those recent events have caused doubt to form in our minds."

That son of a bitch. This was a damned ambush.

"We do not wish to challenge you, sire," Vardel continued, "but we cannot keep quiet with what has happened."

"And what, exactly, is it that you're concerned about?" Keddrick ground out. "Gravaick did not win that night. As a matter of fact, neither side won. We both lost many men. Through it all, my men and I never gave up. The Dráguns are the ones who fled. It isn't as if this is the first time that we've fought them—and this isn't the first time they've retreated."

"You misunderstand me, sire. That is not the event we are most concerned with."

Larken could see that Keddrick had had about enough. Hell, even he was ready to pound the prick into the floor.

"Then what, pray tell, is it you're referring to?" Keddrick's hands clamped down on the arms of the chair, and Larken could hear the wood creaking beneath his grip.

The corner of Vardel's lip pulled up slightly. "You let the coven fall under attack, did you not?"

Larken was halfway across the room when Keddrick said, "Stop."

Stop? Stop! He wants me to stop! He glared at Vardel as he backed up then took his spot next to his sire.

Controlled rage rolled off Keddrick in waves. The room heated with the fire in his stare. The silence was deafening as he slowly stood. "You have chosen your words poorly, Vardel." The powerful calmness of Keddrick's deep voice was unnerving. Even the hairs on Larken's arms stood on end.

The eyes in the room flickered back and forth between Keddrick and Vardel. The shocked faces of the other chancellors only heightened the nervous energy in the air.

The look in Vardel's eyes reflected that he knew he'd made a mistake, but the damn confident expression on his face just showed how arrogant he truly was. "My apologies, again, sire. I seem to be fumbling my words tonight." He straightened his posture. "What I meant to say was that it was unfortunate that the coven was ambushed."

Larken clenched his fists at his sides, ready to beat the man to a bloody pulp. These obscene attacks were going too far, and one more slip-up from Vardel and Larken would be showing the man exactly what it felt like to die.

"If you cannot keep a courteous tongue, then I suggest you find someone else to speak for you," Keddrick warned.

As if it were possible to stand up straighter, Vardel lifted his chin in obvious hopes of showing no fear.

But he should be afraid.

"Now"—Keddrick took his seat again—"what are you getting at?"

"Well." Vardel cleared his throat. "The council and I are well aware that you have run the coven for centuries, but we fear..." His words died off as Keddrick's eyes narrowed. "We are concerned that...that your time as our sire..." Glancing around the room, Vardel quickly sought out support from the others. Most of the men and a few of the women held firm gazes with him, silently urging him on. Which, apparently, was all he needed. Vardel smiled. "You were elected for your position—"

"I earned it," Keddrick growled out.

"That may be so, but we cannot sit idly by and watch the coven fall." Vardel casually made his way to the front of the room again. "It may be time that a new sire is needed."

Once again, Larken was ready to wrap his hands around the vampire's throat, but Keddrick's hand on his arm had him stilling his forward march.

Keddrick eyed Vardel. "You think I cannot run my coven?"

"Trust me, sire. This is not an accusation I am wanting to make."

Yes it is, you asshole.

"But you cannot blame us for our concern about your leadership. You and your warriors are the ones who are supposed to be protecting us. Yet for the last hundred years you have managed to fail at slaying our one true enemy. Gravaick and his Dráguns have killed too many of our people, and then recently managed to trick you into abandoning the coven so they could attack." He sneered when Keddrick frowned. "Yes, I spent part of the day talking with Varek. He has told me all about it."

"Then I assume he told you of how Gravaick's men failed—that they did not seize control of the coven. My mate was the one who stopped them."

"Ah, yes, your mate. I'm glad you mentioned him, because that is another concern we have." Vardel clasped his hands behind his back, not seeming worried at all at the deathly glare in Keddrick's eyes. "I find it...insulting, actually, that you have yet to introduce your mate to us. He is, after all, supposedly running the coven alongside you. So, don't you think that he is a man of importance to our people? Don't you think that we should have a say? I mean, don't you think it only right that we meet him?"

"As you know, free time isn't something I get a whole lot of," Keddrick replied. "I had planned on introducing you to him *after* we had settled this war between us and the Dráguns."

Vardel slightly shook his head and waved a hand dismissively through the air. "That is neither here nor there at the moment. Our main issue is that we are losing faith in your leadership, and we do not like that."

Larken was actually taken back by the boldness of that statement. It was as if the chancellor had no regard for his life whatsoever. His bold words practically signed his death warrant, in Larken's eyes.

Letting out a deep breath, Keddrick relaxed back into his seat. "All right, I see what you are saying."

Larken whipped his head around to stare in disbelief at his sire. "What?"

Keddrick just raised his hand, further silencing any outburst Larken was ready to give. "They have every right to question my authority, Larken. If I were them, I would do the same. The problem," he said to Vardel, "is that none of you are there to see what goes on. You have no idea what it is that we are doing. You only base your judgments on what others tell you. You do not see the way I run my coven, so you do *not* have the right to accuse me of being unworthy of my role."

That stupid grin tugged at the corners of Vardel's mouth again.

"I completely agree, sire. As a matter of fact, that was what we were all thinking. And I believe I have a solution for that."

Keddrick's eyebrow rose again. "And that is?"

Casually strolling around the room again, Vardel said, "You are in need of warriors at the coven, yes?"

"You already know we are," Keddrick relied sternly.

"That is good, because I think I can help. You see, I have felt that it was only right that I do everything I can to help protect our people as well. So, over the years I have brought together a group of men that have served as protectors to our city." He stopped his wandering and faced their sire. "They have been trained, just as your warriors have. Their commander is quite an excellent swordsman."

"Is that so?" Keddrick said drily.

A flash of annoyance crossed the chancellor's face, but faded quickly. "Yes, that is so," he replied derisively. "As I was saying, since you are in need of men, and we are in need of assurance, then I think — and the council agrees — that my men will join the coven and the commander will report back to me. He is a trustworthy and fair man who has quite a sense of nobility, so I assure you that he will not twist his findings in any way. The council will hear honestly of what goes on at the coven."

The room fell silent once again. Larken thought the entire idea was preposterous, and thought his sire would be crazy for even taking the man's suggestions. It was obviously a ploy — one that he knew would not end on a good note.

"And how many men is it that you have?"

"Including the commander? Seven."

Keddrick stared Vardel down. "I'd like to meet this commander you speak so highly of."

A smile stretched out over the chancellor's face. "I believe you've already met him," he answered, gesturing to the main entrance of the room while keeping his gaze locked with Keddrick's.

The butler took his cue and opened the door, and Larken stared baffled at the man that entered.

"My son, Khale."

Vardel's tone was like ice through Larken's veins, but even the chill quickly subsided, replaced by the numbness that spread through him.

Then, as if the entire thing was a cosmic joke, Larken could do nothing but choke back the laughter that threatened to burst out of him. From the look on Khale's face, it was clear that he'd heard his father's words through the door, and it was equally clear that he hadn't the slightest idea that Vardel had planned this.

At least he hoped that Khale hadn't known. His humor died off just as quickly as it had come. *If that boy accepted me into his bed in hopes of cozying up to me for information on bringing Keddrick down, then he can think again.*

Khale tried his hardest to keep his shocked expression under control, but he hadn't had much time to recuperate from his father's words before the door had opened for him. It was unbelievable what his father was trying to do, and he wasn't quite sure he agreed with it, but his mind couldn't get past the fact that his father was entrusting him with something so important.

So this was what he was talking about earlier? This is what he wanted me for?

Hope swelled inside him. This was his chance, his opportunity to show his father that he was loyal to him and that all he'd ever wanted was... Well, love might be too soon for Vardel, but maybe the man would at least acknowledge him in the future.

The rest of the meeting passed quickly. Keddrick certainly didn't seem too happy about the situation, but he didn't argue against it either. It was nerve-racking having so many people glance his way as they discussed how Khale and his men would join the coven in three days' time — since this would be news to his men as well, Khale was insistent that they have at least tonight to get any affairs in order. Some of the men had wives and children, and he couldn't very well drag them away at a moment's notice.

So Keddrick and Larken would leave tonight, and Khale and his men would follow tomorrow. *Simple, right?*

Khale swallowed past the lump in his throat as he continued to avoid Larken's gaze. He'd been able to feel the man's eyes on him since he had entered the room. With what had happened between them, he was sure that things would be a little uncomfortable in the beginning, but was hopeful that it would ease over time. He was determined to do right by his father. He wasn't going to let the tryst between him and the warrior mess that up.

He finally risked a glance at the handsome man when the meeting concluded. Those striking blue eyes pierced his and Khale immediately looked away. He couldn't help but be curious as to what Larken thought about all of this.

When the meeting came to a close, Khale politely said his farewells to everyone then left. He had a lot to do tonight to prepare for tomorrow's departure. He'd never spent more than a couple of days away from home, so he was a little nervous about that, but he pushed his anxiety aside.

He'd admit that when growing up he hadn't been the most well-behaved son. He'd idiotically thought that he could gain his father's attentions by acting out. But once he'd turned fifty he'd realized that he was coming at it from the wrong angle. His father wanted strength, power and loyalty, and Khale had worked very hard since, trying to give him just that.

Chapter Five

Larken was pretty sure his frown hadn't left his face since they'd left the chancellors the previous evening. Even the licus wasn't enough to lighten his mood. His mind had been flooded with nothing but thoughts of Khale—his hair, the incredible color of his eyes, the sound of his voice, the way the man's body felt beneath his. Most importantly, though, was the never-ending pensive feeling that Khale was going to get under his skin his entire stay here.

"How can you let them do this?" Wesley asked, pulling Larken from his thoughts.

Keddrick relaxed into the high-backed chair across from Larken. "I don't really have a choice."

Wesley gave him an almost disgusted look. "But you're the sire, you're above them all!"

Remus caressed his mate's arm and Wesley leaned into the touch. "Calm down, love," Remus said softly.

"That may be, Wesley," Keddrick replied. "But they still have a say. They can still sway any decisions made here. Normally, the council leaves everything up to the sire, but that doesn't mean they don't have

the ability to overrule any decisions the sire makes."
When the little blond scowled, Keddrick continued,
"You know, your government is fairly similar to the
way we operate here. Think of me as the President,
and Vardel as the Vice President, and so on. In the
case of national security or unlawful acts, they can
impeach the President if they want."

"I still don't think it's fair."

"Well, thank you for being on my side, but you have
to remember, I agreed to this—they didn't force it
upon me. I may not like it, but I understand where
they're coming from."

"I still say we be on our top guard," Larken cut in. "I
don't have a good feeling about Khale and his *merry
men* joining us."

"I don't understand how it's possible for Khale to
even be a commander," Remus said astonishingly.
"Last time I saw him he was a skinny, whiney,
sniveling little brat."

Larken couldn't help but chuckle. "Oh, trust me, he
may be a brat still, but he's anything but skinny and
whiney. Well, don't quote me on the whiney part yet,
but skinny for sure doesn't fit his description." He
thought back to their last conversation they'd had in
Khale's room. "He's pompous and stuck up, though."

His sire looked bemused as he regarded Larken. "I
didn't know that you'd had time to get to know him."

Holding a steady gaze, Larken replied, "We ran into
each other in the hallway and got to talking." *Well, it's
the truth.* Granted, they really hadn't done all that
much talking over their time spent together, but there
had still been words exchanged—just none that
Larken felt like sharing with everyone.

That put a smile on his face. He had never really
been a dominant person in bed, but there was

something about Khale that had him wanting the man to bend to his every whim. Khale was nearly as tall and strong as he was, but Larken had wanted complete control. It had irked him that Khale had moved when he'd been told to stay still, but at the same time Larken had kind of liked the fact that Khale had disobeyed, had fought back.

Larken glanced over to Zane, who sat comfortably holding his mate. He wondered why it had never been like that between them. He'd always been submissive to Zane, had always let Zane take him.

He had *wanted* to give himself to Zane.

Larken gave himself a mental shake, forcing his thoughts of their time together out of his head. It was in the past and there was nothing he could do about it now.

It doesn't matter anymore. I've moved on from Zane.

With that thought, Khale was front and center in his mind again. He knew it would be hard to ignore the enticing young man, but he couldn't let what they'd shared continue on at the coven. And it wasn't as if Khale had shown any interest in extending what they had — hell, even Larken didn't want to further it.

Their bed play had been great, though.

Larken forced himself to clear his mind. He really needed to stop thinking about the man. Right now he needed to focus. He needed to… "What?" he asked, when he noticed the others staring at him curiously.

Remus smiled and said, "You had this devilishly pleased-looking grin on your face. What were you thinking about?"

"Yeah," Wesley piped in. "Care to share with the class?"

Larken wiped every emotion from his features. "Nope."

"Anyway," Keddrick drawled out then turned his attention to Remus. "Khale has definitely grown up. He's no longer the little kid you remember. I only hope that he hasn't turned into his father." He looked around the room to the others. "I want you all to be on your best behavior while they're here. You will treat these men as if they were your fellow warriors. Hell" — he tossed one hand in the air — "they *will* be your fellow warriors. They'll be bound in by taking the oath just like every other warrior that's joined the coven. So, please, treat them as such."

There was a series of nods around the room, but no one commented. It was going to be hard to accept the newcomers when these men were being forced on them as they were. The men who joined the coven usually had to prove themselves, prove their worth — not just be given a free pass without question.

Larken only hoped that these men lived up to Vardel's praises.

"How will I know which one is Khale?" Wesley asked.

Remus glanced at his mate. "He'll be the one looking down at you."

Wesley gave him an incredulous look and said sarcastically, "Honey, I'm five-six, everybody looks down at me."

Larken couldn't help but smile at that.

Remus rolled his eyes. "Past the end of his nose, Wesley. I meant —"

Wesley flapped his hand through the air, cutting his mate off. "I know what you meant. Jesus, you have no sense of humor."

Remus just shook his head and rolled his eyes again.

"You have yet to tell me how I'll recognize him."

"Don't worry, Wesley," Larken said. "You can't miss his hair."

Remus leaned forward, resting his elbows on his knees, and looked over to Larken. "The kid does have some interesting hair, doesn't he? I've never seen anything like it."

"That's not very helpful, you know," Wesley said.

"Oh, trust me" — Larken grinned again — "it's all you'll need."

Wesley continued to look back and forth between Larken and Remus, his irritation clearly growing as they remained evasive with him.

"They're never going to tell you," Eli piped in. "So I might as well."

Wesley sat up straighter on the couch. "Thank you, Eli." He playfully smacked Remus' arm. "See, now that's a friend. He doesn't tease me like you." He looked over to Eli. "Okay, tell me."

Eli shook his head and smiled. It was the first time Larken had seen the man smile in he didn't know how long. Eli had been too quiet since they had gathered in the war room. He'd done nothing but stare out of the window. Even now Eli's gaze returned to the view, his smile fading.

"When Keddrick told me about them coming here, he also told me the story about Khale's birth. It was actually big talk back then — the murder of a council member's mate was unbelievable, and still is. Khale's mother had been ill, and Vardel feared for her safety during labor, so he sought out a mage." Eli glanced over to his mate. "Did they ever find out the reason why the wizard did what he did?"

Shaking his head, Keddrick replied, "No, and it wasn't as if the mage had a chance to give it, seeing as

Vardel slit the man's throat shortly after his mate died."

Eli shrugged. "Anyway, there were rumors that just before the childbirth the mage had created a potion to ease the mother's pain. It's said that a flower was added to the mix." He finally gave his attention to the room. "It's also said that white streaks formed in the woman's hair shortly after. I found this to be very strange, so I did a little research. It took me all of yesterday, but I think I figured it out. There is a rare flower that is feared yet treasured at the same time. It's treasured and sought after because it's supposed to be the most beautiful flower in existence. Yet it's feared because it's also the most deadly."

"Deadly?" Wesley asked. His brow scrunched down. "I would've never thought a flower could be deadly. What's it called?"

"*Athis Dey*. It's mage for 'divine beauty'."

"So how do you know that is was that flower that killed her?" Wesley questioned.

Turning to look at the little blond, Eli replied, "Because the flower is the whitest of whites with light violet mixed in."

Wesley frowned. "What does this have to do with Khale's hair?"

"Because the man's hair, as Eli says, is the whitest of whites and has purple streaks running through it," Keddrick answered.

Wesley's jaw dropped. "No way! His hair is white? With purple in it?"

"I believe that's what he just said, love." Remus playfully poked his mate in the side.

"Wow, that is so cool. Oh, I can't wait to see it!"

"Now, Wesley." Keddrick sat forward in his chair, a stern look on his face. "Don't go bugging the man about it. I'm sure he's endured enough with the attention his hair has given him, and my guess is most of the attention wasn't wanted."

Holding his hands up in surrender, Wesley said, "Okay, okay, I won't say anything." A grin formed, lighting his eyes up with mischievousness. "I can't make any promises that I won't be staring. I mean, come on—white and purple hair? That's gonna be hard not to look at."

The little blond was right about that. It was hard not to stare, but for Larken he didn't think it was all because of his hair. There was something unique about the young man's looks. He was stunning, his features flawless. Larken pondered on the flower's name. *Divine beauty, huh?* A vision of Khale filled his mind and he couldn't help but think that it fit him perfectly. Maybe that was what had him so drawn to Khale.

Just then the door opened and Gabe stepped inside. "They're almost here. Savino spotted them about a quarter of a mile away."

"Thank you," Keddrick said, then raised his hand, dismissing Gabe. He glanced around the room. "And it begins."

They all made their way down to the entrance hall, where the other warriors had already gathered. It was strange to see so many new faces among them. Usually, new warriors trickled in over the years—to have fifteen new men join in such a short period of time... *Gods, I can't even remember all of their names, and now there are going to be seven more.*

"Everyone, look alive," Keddrick ordered. "They're here."

Larken couldn't help but notice how his heartbeat kicked up a notch. *Probably just from the anxiety of this stupid situation. They shouldn't be here.* It took a lot for him to keep a stoic expression on his face. He wasn't ready to show them how much this pissed him off.

And how much it scared him that he'd actually missed Khale a little.

But what is there to miss? I barely know the guy.

The coven doors opened and several large men marched in.

The hackles rose on the back of Larken's neck. The men immediately gave off the persona as if they were better than everyone else — including Khale.

"Wow, look at his hair," Wesley blurted out.

"*Hush,*" Remus chided.

Wesley stood wide-eyed and with his mouth slightly parted as the men came farther into the hall. "He looks like an anime character out of a *yaoi* manga."

Eli let out a sudden snort then quickly covered his mouth with his hand to hide his smile.

"A what?" Remus asked.

Wesley opened his mouth to speak, but Eli quickly said, "Nothing. It's not really something to talk about right now." He raised his eyebrows and gave Wesley a pointed look.

With his gaze never leaving Khale, Wesley tilted his head to the side and continued on, "Yet he looks like an English gentleman at the same time."

"Wes!" Eli chided.

Wesley looked at Eli. "Some of his clothes... They'd be like the Regency era, right?"

"*Wesley,*" Eli said a little more harshly.

Wesley ducked his head, but his grin held firm. "Sorry."

Larken couldn't blame Wesley for the reaction he had, because Khale was quite a sight. Sure, his hair was like something never seen before, but he also held a power of superiority and strength when he walked. And it wasn't just Khale. His men also had a dark and dangerous vibe to them. He could tell they truly were warrior material. Yet he had a feeling that Khale and his men knew they weren't really welcome here — at least not under these pretenses — and he was sure that they felt they'd need to make a name for themselves.

With his shoulders back and a sure expression on his face, Khale entered the coven. The warmth inside was a pleasant welcome from the bitter cold, but the uninviting looks on the warriors' faces sent a chill down his spine. Going into this mission, he knew that there would be bumps along the way, one being that they may not be accepted, but he wasn't about to let that deter him. Khale was going to do everything in his power to earn their trust. He wanted them to know that he was here to be *with* them, not against them.

That his father had basically forced Keddrick to allow him and his men into the coven surely didn't sit well with the warriors, who all had to prove themselves and work hard to join. Yet Khale was ready to show them that he and his men had trained hard and were just as worthy.

Against his will, Khale's gaze sought out the one man he knew he'd have the hardest time working with. Larken stood near the back with Keddrick and Remus, his arms crossed over his chest and a firm expression over his features. The man was just as captivating and handsome as he remembered. With a square jaw, high cheekbones, and a set of clear blue eyes one could get lost in. He was mesmerizing.

Stop staring, you idiot.

Turning his attention to Keddrick, he crossed the entrance hall and stopped before him. Bowing, he said, "Sire, thank you again for allowing us to join you."

"Yes, well, it'll be nice to have more men," Keddrick replied.

Not quite the answer he was hoping for. Then again, he didn't really expect a joyful welcome.

"There's a lot of people to try to introduce, so I'll just let you all do that on your own," Keddrick said. "But there are a few of my men I'd like you to meet now, seeing as you'll be working more closely with them." Keddrick gestured to a man farthest to Khale's right. "At the end there is Zane. You and your men will be working with him the most with training."

Khale walked down to greet him and was slightly stunned by the scar on his face, but felt that he did a well enough job of hiding his shock. He'd heard of Zane before—of how unpleasant a vampire he was—and Khale hadn't been looking forward to meeting him. He had a feeling that Zane was going to be the hardest to work with.

"Zane," Khale acknowledged as he held out his hand. "It's a pleasure to meet you."

The man stared him down before he slowly reached out and grasped his hand in return and nodded. Khale quickly glanced to the man next to Zane, then did a double take and could do nothing but stare. Amber eyes gazed back up at him. "You're a dragon," he blurted out, immediately feeling like a fool afterwards.

The dragon smiled up at him. "You're very observant."

Khale felt his cheeks heat with embarrassment.

Zane's arm came up and wrapped around the dragon's shoulders. "This is my mate. Do you have a problem with that?"

His mouth opened and closed several times before Khale finally sputtered out, "N-no, of course not. I just... I just..." He let out a flustered sigh. He was making himself look like a mumbling idiot. "My apologies." He held his hand out. "My name is Khale. It's nice to meet you."

The dragon shook his hand. "I'm Boek, but, please, call me Bo."

"And you live here?" Khale stifled another sigh. He could not believe he'd asked that. He so badly wanted to close his eyes and shake his head at his ridiculous behavior, but instead tried his hardest to keep a steady expression.

Bo smiled and chuckled. "Yes, I live here. And so does my brother."

This surprised Khale even further. *There are two of them living here?* All right, he could understand why Bo was here, but he was curious as to why his brother was as well. *Something to check into*, he noted to himself. He wondered if this was something his father would want to know about.

The clearing of Keddrick's throat brought him back from his thoughts. "As I said, you'll be training the most with Zane, but you'll also train with Damien. Right now Damien is out, so you'll meet him later." He gestured to Larken then. "You two have already met, but for the rest of you" — he looked past Khale to his men — "this is our Second Commander, Larken."

There was a series of grunts of acknowledgment from behind him.

Any words of greeting Khale had lodged in his throat. Larken's hard gaze had him pausing. The man's stare was intense, yet beautiful at the same time. The sky blue color cut through him, leaving him speechless. His cock began to stir, and the thought of being embarrassed by getting an erection in front of all of the men had him quickly stepping to his left to greet the next man in line.

"Ah, Remus," he said with a smile. "It has been years, has it not?"

Remus clutched his hand and shook it firmly. "That it has. And look at you—all grown up, I see."

Khale grinned. He had only met Remus once many years ago, but he had taken an immediate liking to the man. Looking back now, he felt silly about how in awe he'd been of Remus. From the first moment he'd met him all those years ago, Khale had been able to tell that Remus was genuine. He'd idolized and looked up to the older vampire—more so than he had with his own father at the time. Remus had held a sense of sureness and power that you just didn't see anymore, and meeting him again, Khale could still feel it radiating from him. Khale hated that he'd acted like such a spoiled child when they'd met. He hoped that Remus would come to see him differently now.

"This is my mate, Wesley," Remus announced.

Khale smiled down to the little blond at the commander's side. "Hello."

Wesley just stared at him for a moment, a look of wonder on his face, before he finally said, "Your eyes are purple."

Khale barked out a laugh, while Remus chided his mate.

"I'm sorry. I'm sorry," Wesley said. "But come on, you didn't tell me his eyes were friggin' purple!"

"Wesley!"

Khale chuckled and said, "It's quite all right. This isn't anything new to me." He smiled at Wesley.

"They're so beautiful," the blond said in amazement.

Remus' hand came to rub his forehead. "My gods, Wesley, please stop," he grumbled.

Laughing again, Khale waved the whole thing off. "Again, I'm used to this." He turned his attention to Remus' mate. "Thank you."

Finally, he stood before his sire again.

Keddrick placed his hand on the shoulder of the man next to him. "And this here is Eli, my mate."

Khale bowed then shook the man's hand. "It's an honor to meet you," he said respectfully. Eli nodded and smiled and Khale sensed a power flowing from him. There was something different about this man, and he was eager to learn what it was.

Stepping back and gesturing to his men, Khale said, "I'd like to introduce you all to Ile, my second in command, and our men Jade, Baley, Arra, Ojett and Phine."

There was a series of grunted acknowledgments, but no one moved to shake hands. *Gods, this might be harder than I thought.* If he didn't get his men to at least be civil with the warriors, he feared that Keddrick might cut their stay short and kick them out. And going home to his father empty-handed was not an option.

"It is a pleasure to meet you all," Keddrick said, "but I unfortunately must say, Ile, that while you may have been Second Commander with your little group, at the coven Larken is Second Commander. While you all are here, you'll be joining the warriors in the bottom ranks, just like everyone else."

Khale tried hard not to wince at the unpleasant expression on Ile's face, but fortunately the man remained silent. "We understand," Khale quickly added. The last thing he needed was for his men to create a fuss. Yes, it sucked, but they'd get their statuses back when they returned to Allengard.

"Excellent." Keddrick gestured for them to follow him.

They walked through the coven, everyone remaining silent, until they reached a room that left Khale in awe. Rich colored fabrics and tapestries covered the walls. Candles lined every available surface, giving the area a warm ambience. A bowl of herbs smoked in the corner, its deep, musky scent filling his senses. The space was large but simple, and he felt miniscule compared to the power and strength the room radiated. At the far end stood an altar with an open book upon it. After walking over to get a closer look, he noticed dozens of names inscribed along the left page, and half filling the right.

"This is the Sidulv room, also known as the binding room," the sire informed them. "If you men are truly serious and ready to dedicate yourselves to this coven, then we'll proceed." He walked over to stand beside the book. "You will each swear an oath then sign your names into the daya. This book holds the name of every warrior that has served here." He looked to Khale and his men. "Are you ready?"

Khale swallowed hard, but kept his voice steady as he repeated the words of honor and service he pledged to his people. As he wrote his name in the daya, he couldn't help but think that it looked awkward there, yet somehow fitting at the same time.

Khale had been part of a protective group back in Allengard, but here... Here he felt as if it truly meant something.

He turned to his men to see if they showed any expression of feeling the same, and his heart sank. The deadpan looks on their faces told him they probably didn't. This was just a mission to them — some had even expressed it to him before they'd left home.

This had to have been hard for Keddrick — allowing men to join such a sacred group because Vardel had pushed it on him. He knew that the sire was only doing this to pacify the council. Khale wondered if it would help ease Keddrick to know that he truly meant to do right by joining them.

And yet you're going to spy for your father?

Khale ignored the voice in his head. He wasn't going to spy. He was simply going to record his findings and pass them along. He didn't believe Keddrick was doing anything wrong, and he knew it wouldn't be long before the council realized it as well. His father had been doing nothing but filling the other chancellors' heads with misguided accusations. Khale knew they'd see what was right sooner or later.

"If you will" — Keddrick regarded the warriors in the room — "I will speak with our new members alone. Thank you all for witnessing this moment."

Khale stood still as the room emptied, watching Larken leave out of the corner of his eye.

Once only he and his men remained, Keddrick made to step forward, but Eli placed a hand on his arm. "If I may?"

Keddrick nodded and Eli walked forward to stand before them. "We welcome you to the coven. You each are one of us now and we hope that you'll take this position seriously. In the end, though, no matter where or who you serve, you have but one purpose — to protect our people. The vampires of this world are in need of your help. Times are dire right now with the threat of Gravaick, and we hope that you'll do everything you can to help remove that danger." He began to pace. "Also, while you may be a part of this coven, we do realize that this is something you're not accustomed to. You are used to working within your group, but you must realize now that you'll have to open that shield and work with the others. Working as one is the only way this coven can run smoothly. Singling your group out will only ruffle the camaraderie this coven holds."

Eli ceased his pacing and stopped next to Keddrick. Before, Khale hadn't gotten the impression that Eli held much stature here, but seeing and hearing him now was changing that opinion.

"On another note," Eli continued, "there is one big thing you must adhere to. While the coven is a housing and training ground for the warriors, it is first and foremost our home, and you will treat it as such. We each live our lives here, and are very settled in our ways. Showing off to prove yourselves will get you nowhere. While the men may be warriors, they are humble men, and you'll do right to respect everyone and everything within these walls, just as they do." He eyed each of them. "We are welcoming you into our home. Please, do not disrespect us."

Khale was happy to see that his men nodded in acknowledgement. He only hoped that they meant it as much as he did.

Chapter Six

Damien sighed as he stared at the castle at the east end of the dragon village. He was getting tired and was cold as hell.

"He's not here."

Damien jolted at the warm breath against his ear. Taking a step away, he gave Nikolai an irritated look. "He has to be."

Rolling his eyes, Nikolai said, "No, he doesn't—and he's not."

"Well, it's the last damn place we've got."

"Yes, and it's the last damn place he'd go. Besides"—Nikolai waved a hand toward the castle down the hill from them—"we've been watching that place for a couple of hours now and have seen no sign of Gravaick or the others, just a few dragons coming and going."

"They could be his servants."

Nikolai shook his head. "He wouldn't have servants this soon. He'd take a lot more time to make sure they were secure before he allowed outsiders in like that.

And, again, he would never choose a place this close to Sarren."

Damien whirled around to glare at him. "Then what do you suggest we do? Because we've checked every other damn castle within the dragon countries. He couldn't have just disappear into thin air." He looked back down to the castle. "Maybe he's in the regular homes in a village."

"No, that would never work. He wouldn't take the chance of spreading his men out like that. He's only got like...what, fifty men left? He'd want them close."

Gritting his teeth, Damien ground out, "Well, maybe you don't know him as well as you thought you did, otherwise you would know where the hell he'd be hiding out."

Nikolai came to stand next to him. "He never mentioned anything. All he ever talked about was one day taking the coven." He looked to Damien. "But believe me, I had no idea when that was going to happen."

Damien shook his head. "I believe you. I just can't believe you don't know where his back-up hide out would be."

Nikolai frowned at him. "You know, he didn't tell me everything. In so many words I'd made it clear to him that I didn't like him and didn't really want anything to do with him."

"Then why did he want you back so badly?"

Looking off into the distance, Nikolai replied, "I don't know, and I'm not sure I want to. I saw the look in his eyes—the possessiveness was eerie." He turned back to Damien and smiled. "But I have no intentions of ever joining him again." He winked at him. "I'm happy just where I am."

With his brow pulled down, Damien eyed him. He wasn't too fond of the way Nikolai was paying so much attention to him lately. Hell, ever since the Drágun had come to the coven, Damien felt...different. Every time Nikolai was around him, it was as if Damien was standing on his tiptoes, ready to jump out of his skin at any moment. The more he was around the man the easier it was, but he still wasn't fond of it.

He glanced back over to Nikolai, momentarily mesmerized by the bright silver of his eyes, which appeared almost to glow. When they were around others, Nikolai's eyes would be the usual solid black of all other Draguns. Keeping the secret that he and his brother were a part of the Airos clan had to be hard for Nikolai, but having the ability to perform magic to hide his Airos side was incredible. Damien still couldn't believe that Nikolai was part mage. And he liked that every time they were alone together, Nikolai changed the color of his eyes from black to the original silver they should be.

I wonder why he does that? Does he do it when he's alone with the few others that know his secret? What would happen if others found out? Would he be hunted like his people were all those years ago? And why would so many people be afraid of the Airos clan? Just because they're mixed breeds of vampires, dragons, mages and humans doesn't mean they're bad people.

Damien halted his thoughts and cleared his head. He didn't even know why he would wonder about something like that. It wasn't as if he cared. He wasn't *supposed* to care. If he wasn't careful, he was going to find himself falling for the man, and that was something he couldn't do. Nikolai was a Drágun—and then some—and he didn't quite know why, but

Damien had a feeling that nothing good would come of it. "Come on," he grumbled as he headed away from the village. They were wasting their time. Gravaick obviously wasn't there. After mounting their horses, they started an easy pace back to the coven.

They traveled along in silence for a bit before Nikolai randomly said, "You know, I like this." He motioned between the two of them. "It's much more fun searching for Gravaick with you than it was with Ballen last night. Gods, last night was *so* boring."

Damien noticed the hint of sarcasm in his voice. "Is that so?" he mumbled.

"Yeah. Last night all we did is talk, talk and talk. He told me some things about him. I told him a few things about me. We laughed a few times. Boring!" The sarcasm dripped from every word that time. He smiled at Damien. "It's much more fun with you."

Damien refused to acknowledge the Drágun's bantering. For most of the night they'd remained silent. He didn't really feel like he had anything to say to Nikolai. Since meeting him, every time Damien opened his mouth to speak, he felt as though he was going to spill some sort of personal information about himself for no odd reason. So, he kept quiet most of the time.

Nikolai suddenly stopped his mare. "Hey, what's that?" Dismounting, his feet then crunched in the snow as he walked off the path and into the trees.

Damien frowned. "What are you doing?" He lost sight of him for a moment and his heart began to race. "Nikolai!"

The Drágun popped his head out from around a tree. "There's no need to yell. I'm right here." With a huge grin on his face he said, "Look what I found." He held up the white flower. "A Snow Medda."

The Snow Medda was the only flower known to bloom in winter. How the thing survived the cold was beyond him. He was surprised, though, that Nikolai had seen the thing among the snow that dusted over everything.

Nikolai walked back onto the path then mounted his horse. He held the flower up as if admiring it then he glanced over to Damien.

Goose bumps spread over Damien's arms. Narrowing his eyes, he warned, "Don't even think about it." Nudging his steed in the sides, he started home again.

Nikolai quickly caught up to him. "Why not? It would be a shame not to share this. It's such a beautiful flower."

"Yeah, one you'd give to a beautiful woman."

There was a brief moment of silence. "Or a handsome vampire," Nikolai replied, his voice sultry and warm.

Damien's hands tightened around the reins. "No," he growled out.

He didn't have to look at Nikolai to sense the shift in the air. Taking a sideways glance at the Drágun, Damien noted that his posture had stiffened and his expression had become stoic.

Oh, for crying out loud. Rolling his eyes, Damien guided his horse closer to Nikolai's. Reaching out, he snatched the flower from the man's hand then put space between them once again. Taking a quick glance at the stunning blossom, he then tucked it away in a pocket within the folds of his cloak.

"You'll squish it that way," Nikolai commented. When Damien glared at him, Nikolai raised a hand in surrender. "I took the damn flower, didn't I?"

A soft smile fell over Nikolai's features. "Yes, you did."

Nikolai turned his attention to the road ahead of them and Damien did the same, but he didn't miss the quiet "Thank you" the man murmured.

Damien ignored it and continued their trek. He was cold and tired and just wanted to lie down. But he knew he probably wouldn't be able to, seeing as they were getting new warriors in. He wished he could've been there when they'd first arrived, but the search for Gravaick didn't pause for anyone. The Drágun was a bigger threat than ever and they needed to find him.

* * * *

Walking across his room, Larken swallowed down the bitter licus leaf — he didn't think he'd ever get used to the taste. After pouring himself a drink, he was on his way to the couch when a knock sounded at his door.

"Come in." He plopped down on comfy cushions and slowly sipped the liquor. Looking over to the doorway, he watched as Corben entered then closed the door behind him. "Hey," he acknowledged.

The vampire came to a stop next to the couch. "Hi."

After a long moment of silence, Larken finally gave in and asked, "What can I do for you?"

Corben glanced toward the fire and slightly shook his head. "Nothing. Just came by to talk."

Talk — yeah right. "So, then talk," he said as he stood to go get himself another drink. Facing Corben again, Larken brought the cup to his lips and downed half of its contents in one gulp, relishing the burning feeling it caused.

"So," Corben said languidly, "this is something else, yeah? I mean, having these new guys come here."

Larken just shrugged his shoulders.

Corben's eyes darkened as he looked off into the distance. "That Khale sure is something."

Larken's eyebrows rose as he stared at the vampire with a smirk. "You like him, do you?"

Corben quickly shook his head. "No. No, not like that. I wouldn't... He seems like the kind that would get attached too quickly."

It was a good thing Corben had brought that up, because Larken had been meaning to talk to the man about that. "And you don't want that?"

Corben snorted and shook his head. "No."

Good. He liked Corben and all, and sleeping with him had been fun, but he didn't want more than that. So it was good to hear that Corben didn't either. Larken looked at him in a whole different light now. He trailed his gaze up and down Corben's body and thought of how much fun they could have together. And the sexy, lustful expression the vampire was giving him suggested he was thinking the same thing.

Corben stepped over to Larken and took the drink out of his hand. After consuming the rest of it, he placed it on the shelf behind him. He stood close — close enough that Larken could feel the heat of his body. Leaning in, Corben placed a soft kiss at the base of his throat. Larken's eyes closed briefly, his head tilting back as Corben's mouth made its way up his neck.

If there was one thing he liked best about Corben, it was the man's mouth. Corben had an intense kiss, and his lips could be so firm around his dick.

Corben grabbed the hem of his tunic, and Larken lifted his arms compliantly. He exhaled on a deep breath when the man latched onto one of his nipples with his mouth. Leaning back against the shelf, Larken pushed his hips forward and ground his erection against Corben's. His skin tingled where Corben's hands ran along his sides and abdomen—the light brush of his fingertips causing goose bumps to spread across his flesh. Suddenly, the vampire's hand was wrapped around the back of his neck and they embraced in a fierce kiss. It was a battle of tongues as they devoured each other's mouths.

As usual, Larken's mind began to wander. With the help of the licus and liquor, his head hummed as he pictured someone else's strong hands on his body. He gripped tightly onto the muscles of the man's back, kneading his fingertips in. Tilting his head to the side, he deepened the kiss—enjoying the taste of him, wanting to feel him in any way he could. Something sparked inside him as he pictured the sculpted frame beneath his hands. He wanted to map out this entire body with his mouth, run his tongue over every bump and curve. Lifting his hands, Larken cupped the vampire's slender face.

Wait. What? Zane doesn't have a slender face.

Opening his eyes, he gasped as a vibrant purple gaze stared back at him. Jerking back, he blinked hard and looked again.

Corben stood there staring at him, a confused look on his face. "What? What's wrong?"

Shaking his head in hopes of clearing it, Larken stepped to the side and out of Corben's reach. "Uh..." He shook his head again then closed his eyes and pinched the bridge of his nose. *What in the hell just happened?* After grabbing his tunic off the floor, he quickly put it back on then looked at Corben. "Um, listen, I'm pretty tired. Maybe you should go."

Corben gaped at him, his eyes widening. "What?" Quickly schooling his features, he put on a sexy smile and stepped closer. "You weren't so tired a minute ago." When he reached out for him, Larken took a step back, and Corben's lustful look faded.

Larken didn't say anything, still too baffled by what he'd seen. Instead, he just stared at Corben then nodded his head in the direction of the door.

Definitely seeming put out, Corben nodded and left.

The second the door closed Larken buried his face in his hands. "What the fuck was that?" he mumbled. He rubbed his eyes then ran his fingers through his hair. Picturing Zane was one thing, but to have Khale come out of nowhere…

Pushing his bewildering thoughts aside, Larken sank down onto his bed. Maybe he *was* tired. He hadn't really gotten any sleep since his last time with Tessa and Corben.

Was that really five days ago?

Time had seemed to blur lately. The days ran together and he'd ghosted through the coven like a wraith — going nowhere, seeming stuck. He felt nothing, yet was so heavy-hearted at the same time. That seemed to bring out the uglier side of him. He knew he had purpose as Second Commander, but he didn't feel like he was doing any good to his men. The new warriors he met earlier today almost seemed to fear him — steering clear of him whenever they could. He wasn't mean to them, but he knew that he had an intimidating persona. He wasn't trying to do it. It just happened.

Larken huffed out a chuckle. It appeared that he'd taken Zane's role among the men — the brooding warrior everyone disliked.

How did this happen? he thought as he rubbed his forehead.

Glaring over to the door when he heard a knock, Larken stomped across his room and yanked the door open. "Damn it, Corben. I told you..." He stopped mid sentence as Khale looked at him with a frown.

"I'm sorry," Khale said. "Were you expecting someone else?"

He could do nothing but stare for a moment. A flutter ran through him—those purple eyes were exactly as he remembered them. It was as if he was seeing them for the first time in years even though he'd left Khale in the Sidulv room only an hour ago.

When Khale raised a questioning eyebrow, Larken quickly spoke, "No, no I wasn't expecting anyone."

A smile spread over Khale's lovely features. "Good, because I was hoping we could talk." When Larken didn't say anything, Khale glanced up and down the hall then back to him. "In private, please."

No, I don't want you in my room. Larken almost growled at his childish thought. He was becoming sick of *himself* with all the Khale this and Khale that nonsense. It was time to go back to not caring.

"Sure." He stepped back and invited the vampire inside.

With his hands clasped behind his back, Khale strolled around the room, assessing everything in it.

"Not quite like back at Daddy's, eh?" Larken asked, his tone dry and unmoving. This one room must seem bleak compared to the suite Khale had back home.

Khale turned to him with a frown. "I'm still not sure how I upset you with my comment the other day, but I didn't come here to talk about rooms again."

Rolling his eyes, Larken walked over to the shelf that held his liquor and poured himself another drink. "So, what did you want to talk about then?"

Khale fidgeted as he clearly searched for words to say. "I, uh... Listen, about the other day, I..." Sighing, he stopped his trek and came to stand before him. "Listen, I don't think we got off too well the other day."

He couldn't stop the grin that tugged at his lips. "Well, I don't know about that. I thought we got off just fine."

With a frown, Khale stared at him confused until Larken's words seemed to finally sink in. "Oh, hell, Larken, I'm not talking about *that*." Khale shook his head and glanced away. "Fine, let me start again. I think we didn't end things on the best of terms."

Larken sighed. He was already confused about what he felt toward Khale, so he really didn't want to talk about what had gone on between them.

With his stare steady on Larken again, Khale continued, "What I'm trying to say is that I know I didn't react the best way with what I said to you. I was being..."

When his pause took too long, Larken offered, "An asshole?"

Khale's face fell to a look of annoyance. "That's not what I was going to say, but yes, an asshole."

Shrugging, Larken downed his drink. "Okay, apology accepted."

With his mouth slightly parted and his eyes widened, Khale stared at him. "I didn't apologize."

"So you're not sorry."

"Well, yes, I am, but don't be so presumptuous and assume that that's what I was going to say."

"But you were."

"That's not the point, I..." Khale gritted his teeth as he glared at him. "Anyway, yes, I'm sorry." He looked to Larken expectantly. After a moment, he asked, "Well, don't you have anything to say?"

Do not care about him, Larken. You've already given your heart away once. No need to chance it again. Push him away.

"No," Larken replied flatly.

"What? You know, you weren't all that fan-fucking-tastic yourself. You were quite rude to me as well." He crossed his arms over his chest and lifted his chin up.

Larken set his drink down and stepped closer. "Yeah, but there's one difference between you and me."

"And what's that?"

He pointed at the younger man. "You care."

That shocked look crossed Khale's features again. "And you don't?"

No, I can't afford to. "No, not really."

Khale just stared at him for a moment then said, "All right, that's fine. Well, I've said my piece, and I hope that things aren't...awkward...between us."

Khale made to leave, but Larken grabbed him by his arm. He didn't know why he stopped Khale, but he just had to. He wanted to push the vampire away, but for some reason watching the man leave wasn't something he could do. *Dear gods, I'm losing my mind.*

"Going so soon?" The words had tumbled from his mouth before he could stop them. *Push him away... Pull him closer...* The thoughts swirled through his mind, making him dizzy. He knew he should keep Khale at a distance, but his body still wanted what he and Corben had started.

"What?" Khale asked.

He turned the young man to face him. Reaching up, he then ran his fingers along Khale's cheek.

"You cannot be serious," Khale said incredulously.

"Why not?" Larken was giving up. He was done fighting his conscience. He leaned in closer and Khale immediately pulled back. Larken froze. "Did you not enjoy our time together the other day?"

Khale's mouth opened and closed several times before he said, "Yes, I did, but that was a mistake."

Larken leaned back. "A mistake?"

Having the space between them now seemed to heighten Khale's confidence. He gently pulled out of Larken's hold and took a step back. "Yes, a mistake, and one I do not intend to repeat."

"Now who's being rude?"

Khale glared at him for a moment. "No matter what I say, it's just going to come out wrong to you, isn't it?"

Larken shrugged his shoulders. "You're the one who said it. I cannot control how you speak. Maybe there's a shortage in the span between your brain and your mouth. Or maybe it's that stick up your ass that's doing the talking for you."

Tilting his head to the side, Khale stared at him. "You hit on me, and then you insult me." Shaking his head, Khale turned and headed for the door. "You obviously have issues, and I don't really care to get mixed up in them."

Larken's gaze was immediately drawn to the end of Khale's thick braid that brushed against the top of his ass as he walked away. *Dear gods, what is it about this man that has me craving him like this?* Khale's comment irritated him, but he still wanted him.

Rushing across the room, Larken spun Khale around and pinned him against the wall. "So which is it? Am I an issue, too low on your society pole, or a mistake?"

Khale's lips pressed tightly together before he replied. "I never said anything about social standing," he ground out. "Whatever excuse you want to go with, then that's what we'll go with. Either way, I do not want it to happen again."

As heated as Khale's words were, Larken could sense the desire growing in the man—the way his eyes darkened, his breath quickening as Larken leaned against him, pressing their bodies firmly together from chest to groin.

Larken quickly dipped his head down to nuzzle Khale's throat. "So, you don't like this?" he whispered as he lightly grazed his lips along the soft skin.

"I..." Khale gasped. "I-I didn't say that."

It had been hard enough to resist Khale before, and hearing that erotic intake of breath and mumbling of words in that sweet accent only fueled Larken more. "Do you not like *this*?" He captured the man's earlobe between his teeth as he ground his erection against Khale's.

Khale shuddered, his body tensing beneath Larken's. "Please, you must stop," he rasped. "I can't... I can't..." Grabbing Larken's biceps, he dug his fingers in. "I'm not supposed to—"

Larken cut off whatever else Khale had to say by kissing him. He nibbled along Khale's bottom lip, reveling in the taste of him. Sliding his tongue along the seam of Khale's lips, he sought entrance. Khale opened to him and their tongues met, swirling together with abandon. Tilting his head to the side, Larken deepened the kiss. He snaked his arms around

Khale and pulled him closer. The taste of him, the very essence of Khale, drove him crazy.

He wanted more.

Larken began to trail kisses along his jaw. "You can't?"

Khale moaned and leaned his head back. "No," he breathed out.

Moving his hands down to grasp Khale's ass, he whispered in his ear, "No?"

Khale cupped the back of Larken's head, holding him there. "N-n..."

Larken pulled away. "No?" he asked more firmly.

Violet eyes stared up at him, confusion and passion clouding them. Khale opened his mouth to speak, but then bit his bottom lip instead.

Larken lowered his head again and gave Khale a chaste yet heated kiss. "Tell me," he ordered as he nipped at Khale's chin.

The young man's arms wound around his shoulders, his hold tight. He shuddered as he hugged Larken. The seconds ticked by as Khale's chest rose and fell with every labored breath. He pressed their cheeks together. "No," he said hoarsely, then released Larken, nudging him away before he slipped out of the room.

Larken stood there staring at the wall, confused as hell, his cock aching in his pants. He was sure that there was no mistaking that Khale wanted him, so why had he left? Swallowing hard, Larken grabbed his dick and squeezed it. He was so turned on—so badly wanting to bury himself deep inside Khale. Memories of that slick, hot channel ran circles through his mind, and his body ached for it.

And Khale *wanted* it. He knew this.

Bracing one hand against the wall, Larken bowed his head, and for the second time that night he asked himself, "What the fuck was that?"

Hadn't he just told himself earlier that he wasn't going to pursue the man? That he didn't want to further it? If it had been any other time—anyone else—he would have brushed the notion off as soon as the other person resisted. But with Khale, he hadn't found it in himself to give up so quickly.

Larken shook his head. *Has to be the licus fucking with me. Damned drug is going to get me into trouble one of these days.*

* * * *

Khale slammed the door to his room closed. Leaning back against it, he took a few steadying breaths. His mind was a haze of emotions and it irritated the hell out of him. After locking the door, he headed into the bathroom. Bracing his hands against the countertop, he looked at his reflection in the mirror. His cheeks were flushed and his lips slightly swollen and red. The light stubble around Larken's mouth had felt incredible against his skin, and he could picture the man grazing his jaw along other sensitive parts of his body.

Shaking his head, he poured water into the basin then splashed some of it on his face. The coolness helped to calm his heated flesh.

He wanted Larken. There was no question about that. He'd never felt this strongly for another man before—not even Emel. But he knew he couldn't have him. Fear of his father's wrath had made him leave Larken's room, but the ache in his chest had him wishing he'd stayed. Khale licked his lips. He could still taste the man. Closing his eyes, he pictured Larken, could feel them pressed together, could feel his breath whisper over his ear, the hardness of the vampire's cock against his. The entire moment had been amazing.

Khale shivered. The very thought of Larken set his lust on fire.

Scrubbing his hands over his face again, he looked back at his reflection. "That was close," he whispered to himself. His heart sank a little as he thought of everything he and Larken could be doing right then, but he focused his mind back on another importance — one that had resurfaced in his conscience when he was in Larken's arms — his father. Sliding his hand around his side and over his back a little, Khale rubbed the tender spot. His rib had finally healed earlier that day, yet it still bothered him sometimes when taking deep breaths.

Then, without thinking, he ran his hand down to cover his now flaccid cock. The pain he'd felt when his father's cane had connected with him there was indescribable, and he never wanted to experience it again.

He didn't know how long he stood there, staring off into nothing as he thought of his father and everything that had happened the other day. He finally exited the bathroom, stripped off his clothes, then crawled into bed and burrowed under the fur blanket. So much of the other day had been amazing, and so much of it horrific. He'd made the worst decision of his life, and had also accepted a chance of a brighter future. Right then, he had nothing. He had no one. It was how his life had usually been, and how it would continue to be if he wasn't careful and couldn't control himself.

He couldn't risk pursuing his attraction to Larken, because he had only one sliver of hope to hold onto — one that he feared was fading — and that was knowing that he had a chance to form a relationship with his father.

Chapter Seven

Larken blinked hard, trying to clear his blurry vision. He had managed a couple of hours of sleep, but thoughts of Khale had stolen what rest he had desperately needed. And it hadn't escaped his knowledge that it was Khale—not Zane—he'd thought of.

Shaking his head, he focused back on what Damien was telling them. His friend and Nikolai had officially confirmed that Gravaick did not reside in the dragon village just to the west of Sarren.

"Well"—Remus drummed his fingers on his desk—"does anyone have any ideas as to where else he might be?"

Larken was ready to suggest that they search the castles again, but seeing Isa stroll into the war room halted his thoughts.

"Hello, gentlemen," she said sweetly.

Keddrick relaxed back in his chair. "I was wondering when you'd come back."

"I was hoping she wouldn't," Wesley mumbled.

Isa scowled at him. "I see I was missed dearly. Well, I hate to burst your bubbles of joy, but I'm not staying. I'm only here to get my things."

"Need help packing?" Wesley piped up.

"Wesley," Remus warned.

"Everyone shut up," Keddrick commanded. Turning his attention to Isa, he said, "I sent you on a task to return something to Barend for me, and you're gone for almost a month. Why?"

Isa pursed her lips. "I do not serve you. While I am happy to help since you are gracious enough to let me stay here, that does not mean you can treat me like one of your men." At Keddrick's rigid look, Isa seemed to think better of how she talked to him. "I passed along your package and then decided to visit for a bit. Then I heard of what had happened with you, Gravaick and the coven, and I thought it best to keep away. I came here for protection, but learning of the breach in the coven... Well, I didn't think it was safe to come back."

"Then why have you?" Larken asked.

She rolled her eyes. "I already told you—to get my things."

"Where will you go?" Remus asked.

Wesley looked to his mate with disgust. "And you care, why?"

The commander frowned, but kept his attention on Isa. "I'm curious."

Giving Wesley a cheeky grin, she replied, "If you must know, while Barend and I share different views on...well, pretty much everything...he has agreed to let me stay with him."

"You are his daughter," Larken added. "It only seems fitting that he'd want to keep you safe."

Isa gave him a droll look. "I doubt that. He only said yes because I promised I'd keep to myself."

"That'd be a first," Wesley snipped out.

Smiling at him coyly, Isa strolled over to where Wesley sat at the large table. "Ah, sweet Wesley, I think I'll miss you the most." She batted her eyelashes at him. "Won't you miss me?"

Wesley narrowed his eyes. "Who would miss a pebble in their shoe?"

"All right, that's enough," Remus ordered harshly.

Wesley ducked his head then leaned against his mate. "I'm sorry."

A steaming looked etched across Isa's features. "Well, I'd best be going then."

"Stop." The room stilled as Eli spoke up. "You can't leave."

Larken had forgotten that the man was even there. Eli's silence could be unnerving at times, and to hear him speak up now surprised him.

Giving Eli a displeasing look, Isa asked, "I beg your pardon?"

Eli got up and walked over to stand next to her. "You're fleeing for your safety, right?"

"Well, I don't see it as fleeing," she retorted. "But yes."

Shaking his head, Eli said, "But you won't be. You'll never be safe as long as Gravaick's out there."

She crossed her arms over her chest. "He's your problem, not mine."

"But he *is* your problem. I won't lie. The vampires are having a hard time defeating him, and I wonder what it is you'll do if the coven ultimately fails in the end? Do you think Gravaick will just stop there? Who do you think he'll go after next?" Before she could reply he pointed at her. "You, and others like you. All of the mages will be next to go."

"Hey, you're a part of that crowd too."

"Yes, and I'm willing to fight with them, which is what you need to do."

Isa's eyes widened. "Me?"

"Yes! And all of the other mages." Eli threw his hands up in the air. "Why is it they've stood by idly this whole time? I refuse to believe our people are dense enough not to have thought of this."

"You want us to fight?"

"Again, yes."

Shaking her head, Isa began to walk away. "I don't think so."

"I said stop!"

Isa froze in her tracks. She wasn't the only one that seemed a little surprised by Eli's commanding voice. This was a side of the human Larken had never seen before.

"How can you do this?" Eli asked. "How can you walk away? If we fight together, then our chances of defeating Gravaick are incredible. Why haven't the mages come forward to help?"

Isa turned back and stared at him. "We prefer to keep to ourselves."

Larken watched as the muscles along Eli's jaw twitched.

"Well, if the vampires fail, then I'm sure Gravaick will be happy to leave you be…for a while, I imagine."

Isa seemed to ponder over Eli's words, her expression becoming glummer. Finally, she sighed heavily and grumbled, "You're right."

Eli's eyebrows rose. "Oh, don't look at me that way." She batted her hand at him. "I'm not stupid. *We're* not stupid. We know that we are most likely next, but like most mages, we choose to avoid confrontation."

"So you're purposefully ignoring impending danger?" Larken asked in disbelief. "What will you do if that danger finally comes?"

Isa shrugged.

"You'll fight," Eli answered.

She let out a frustrated growl. "Yes, I suppose we will. But I can't see it coming to that. I'm sure the vampires will do well enough and take care of Gravaick themselves."

"That's not good enough," Eli replied. "They need to fight now. It's an advantage that Gravaick will never see it coming."

"Is that so? And who do you suppose is going to convince them to join the fight?"

Eli gestured to her.

"Oh, dear man, you have lost your mind." Isa laughed. "I know I'm hard to resist, but the mages don't think so highly of me." She tapped her finger against her chin. "I think it needs to be you."

"No," Keddrick cut in. He looked between his mate and the witch. "I'm sorry, but what exactly is it that the mages can do to help us anyway?"

"Are you serious?" Isa asked incredulously. "I know some witches who can channel the thunder from the sky—happily turning you into a crispy vampire. And with but a few words, I could have you thinking you're a two-year-old boy. And him"—she pointed to Eli—"I'm sure he could destroy an entire army with a single thought." She looked to Eli with an exaggerated sadness. "I'm sure it would destroy you in the process, but you'll have died for a good cause."

"Enough." Keddrick rubbed his forehead.

"So you agree," Eli said to her. "The mages can help. So will you speak to them?"

"No."

"What?"

"I told you. They probably won't listen to me. But you, on the other hand…" She eyed Eli up and down. "I hate to admit it, but I think they'll listen to you."

Eli looked confused. "Why me? They don't know me."

"Ah, but they do. They know you're here. They can sense your power. And it is that power that I think will convince them to join. They'll want to meet you. Without even a word being said, a mage can tell a lot about a person within moments of meeting them. You have to show them that your cause is serious, and that their joining the fight will be a benefit."

"Are you sure they'll listen to me?"

Isa nodded. "I'm fairly confident they will."

"Then it's decided. When do we leave?"

"Now hang on a second," Keddrick commanded. "I don't feel comfortable about you traveling around so much with the Dráguns possibly at your back."

"Don't worry," Isa said. "A simple message passed through a cauldron will gather all of the mages together in one place."

"Would that be like sending an email?" Wesley asked.

Eli smiled. "Yes, Wesley, it'd be like sending an email. And I remember reading about something like that in one of my spellbooks. You write a message on a piece of parchment, light it on fire and place it in your cauldron, then with a simple chant, it'll appear in other mages' cauldrons." He turned to his mate. "Since there won't be a lot of traveling, then I shouldn't be gone long."

"I wouldn't be so quick to say that," Isa butted in. "It took the mages almost a year to decide *not* to join the battle that had gone on between the humans from the west and the humans from the east. Who knows how long it'll take them this time."

Keddrick took his mate's hand. "Then I'm going with you."

Eli shook his head. "No, you're needed here."

"You'll need protection," Keddrick insisted.

"I think I've proven I don't. But seeing as I know you won't back down from this, then fine, I'll take one of the warriors with me."

"Zane," Larken blurted out. When the others looked at him questioningly, he added, "He's one of our best fighters. He's quick and his senses are incredible. Not to mention he'll be the only one that'd be able to help if there were to be trouble during the day." He had been surprised that he'd spoken up so quickly. It was hard to say the vampire's name, no less point out his qualities, but he knew that Zane was the right choice. His heart ached at the thought of not seeing the man, but he agreed with Eli. Having the mages on their side would be a huge benefit.

"It's settled then." Eli smiled.

Larken could tell his sire was reluctant to let his mate go, but Keddrick kept his composure and agreed.

* * * *

"It's so beautiful." Khale looked out in awe at Mirror Pond. He'd heard of this place many times, and had always wanted to see it. And when Ballen had been listing off patrols for that night, Khale had volunteered to go with the vampire to patrol the area around Mirror Pond.

Ballen tossed a rock into the water, disturbing its perfect mirror image of the sky above. "This used to be a beautiful place to visit. Now I don't really see it like that anymore," he said dismally.

"May I ask why?"

Dropping the rest of the rocks he held, Ballen turned toward him. "This was where Eveen and Wesley were kidnapped by Gravaick and his men."

Khale had heard of this. Had been told of what had happened to the human and poor vampire. It had pained him to learn of their suffering.

His eyes filling with sorrow, Ballen looked out over the water. "I feel terrible for Aliam. Eveen was not only his mate—she was his *everything*. I'd always thought that if or when I find my mate, I hoped that I could share the same love those two had. Their bonding was inspirational to the heart. I knew Aliam before he met Eveen, and I could see the better man she made him when they got together." Bowing his head, he nudged the dirt with the tip of his boot. "When Eveen was murdered, I think the whole coven mourned more greatly than ever before. She was not only an amazing mate to Aliam, but an amazing person all around. Everyone loved her. And now she's gone."

"Is that why Aliam left?"

Ballen's brow furrowed a little as he said, "Remus never said what the reason for his leaving was, but the others and I are pretty sure that's why. Aliam had taken her death and held it too close to his heart. We could all see it, see how it was eating away at him. In the end, I think he finally realized that his reactions to her death were hurtling him toward the edge. It was consuming him in the worst way."

Khale felt a stab of sadness for the man. "I can only imagine how hard it was for him."

"Yeah. And it must have been hard leaving the coven, but I understand why he did it. Remus said something about him going to live with Eveen's family. I hope he finds peace there."

"Have you found peace with it?" Khale was a little nervous to ask, but he could tell Eveen's death was hard on him as well.

Ballen shook his head. "No, and I don't imagine I will until Gravaick's head is on a spike. That man has created havoc for everyone, and if there is any reason above the others to find him, it's so I can avenge Eveen's death…for Aliam."

Khale had to wonder how strong the couple's love had been for it to affect so many people. He had never found love, and he had to wonder if he would ever find a love that strong. Then the real question would be, with whom? He knew he wanted his father's approval, but he knew he could never find happiness with a woman. Though, as the time passed with him being away from his home, his urge to be in his father's good graces had eased some. He'd never been this independent before and was truly starting to feel like his own man. Did that mean he was ready to find love? With Larken, perhaps?

No. Khale knew he and Larken wouldn't make a good match. They had too many things going against them. Yet the warm feeling inside him every time they were near grew immensely. The man's clear blue eyes were mesmerizing, and he found himself getting lost in them. Memories of Larken's lips on his, on his body, haunted his mind no matter how hard he tried not to think of it. Their time together at his home, the kiss they'd shared last night, the way Larken had stared hungrily at him this evening as they passed in the hall... He could picture himself with this man, wanted him in more ways than he should, but was it wise?

A snap of a twig pulled Khale from his thoughts, and both he and Ballen looked across the pond just in time to see a figure slip back into the woods.

"Drágun," Ballen whispered harshly.

Within seconds, Khale had run around the water and into the trees. He could hear the Drágun racing through the thick brush, and it was then, from the numerous sounds, that he realized there were two of them. He only hoped that there weren't any more.

Ballen was close on his heels, but it was Khale that caught up to them first. The trees thinned out a bit and he got a glimpse of a man's bare back.

Oh no, they're going to shift.

Khale couldn't let that happen. He had to get to them before they flew away. He dug down deep inside himself and pulled every ounce of energy he had to quicken his pace. He practically flew through the woods, catching up to them just in time to see the shift begin.

Launching himself at the Drágun, he wrapped his arms around a thick, scaly neck and felt himself being lifted into the air. He heard Ballen shout "No," but it was too late. Determination set in and he was not letting go. Once they had cleared the tree canopy, he planned to drive his sword through the top of its head. That is, if he could hold on long enough.

The higher they rose, the more the Drágun thrashed about, trying to knock Khale off. Branches whipped at him, slicing at the bare skin of his cheeks. He tightened his grip on one of the spikes protruding from the creature's back, then looked up just in time to see the forest canopy near...and just in time to see the very thick tree branch. He tried to duck, but it wasn't soon enough.

* * * *

Larken observed the others in the entrance hall. He watched as Keddrick and Eli said their goodbyes, the love in their eyes shining brightly. He tried not to look to his right, tried not to see the love of others, but his heart longed too strongly to ignore what was there — what was true. His heart beat faster as he watched Bo wrap his arms around Zane, the dragon burying his face into the man's chest.

How many times had Larken wanted to do the same? How many times had he ached to embrace the man he'd loved?

He looked away and took a deep breath. He couldn't keep going on like this. It was just too hard — and he now knew what he had to do.

Making sure to keep his features neutral, he made his way over to Zane and Bo and they turned their attention to him when he stopped before them. He avoided Bo's gaze, unable to hold strong under the dragon's soft regard.

Swallowing hard, Larken then said, "Zane, a moment, if you will?" He didn't miss the way Bo's arms tightened around his mate. Zane smiled at Bo and gave him a chaste kiss — the simple gesture making Larken's heart ache all the more. But for what? That it was Bo that Zane was kissing and not him? Or that Larken wanted someone to kiss just the same? To hold. To love. To miss when they leave — if only for a little while.

Unable to stand there a moment longer, Larken headed down the hallway, hearing Zane following behind him. They entered the library, its darkness saddening him further. *Everything's always so dark, so empty.*

Zane reached up to light one of the sconces, but Larken stopped him. "Don't." He needed it this way. He needed to feel cloaked by the heaviness of the night. The light from the moons trickling in through the windows created shadows around them. It teased them and brought them closer together, needing to be near to see each other more clearly. He cherished the closeness, because he truly knew he'd never get it again.

"Larken," Zane whispered.

Raising his hand, Larken shook his head. He needed to say this — he had to say it — and he knew he wouldn't be able to if Zane's deep voice clouded his head. Taking a steadying breath, he gazed at the man he'd fallen for so many years ago. His voice was rough, but he forced himself to speak. "Things will never be as they were."

The saddened expression on Zane's face tore at his heart. Larken knew that Zane understood his meaning. For Zane, their friendship could never be as it once was. The precious camaraderie they'd shared had been stronger than any other, and now it was no more. For Larken, it was his love. So many chances he'd had, so many times he'd passed them by. He had been such a fool.

His breath catching, Larken threw his arms around Zane. His body quaked as Zane embraced him in return. Tears gathered in his eyes, blurring his vision, and his chest ached with his heartbreak. Pressing their cheeks together, he whispered, "I will never stop loving you." His tears finally found their freedom, making their journey down his face. It just hurt so much. He'd never wanted it to be this way, but he knew this was how it was meant to be. His chin quivered as he fought for words. Squeezing his eyes shut, he leaned into Zane. "But I know I have to let you go. I need to let you go." And as hard as it was, he said, "I *want* to let you go."

Zane's arms tightened around him, his chest trembling against Larken's.

I will never have this man in my arms again. But that's all right, isn't it?

With every ounce of strength he had, Larken pulled back. He gazed into Zane's shining eyes, wishing so badly that he could get lost in them as he used to. But it wasn't his right to, not anymore.

That right belonged to someone else now.

Reaching up, he cupped the side of Zane's face, feeling the wetness of the vampire's tears against his skin. Sucking in a shuddering breath, Larken caressed Zane's cheek with his thumb. "He was meant for you," he whispered.

Zane's eyes closed, a new rain of tears flowing down. When he met Larken's gaze again, Larken could see the hurt and happiness in those stunning dark blue orbs. Time stood still as they stared at each other. The seconds ticked by like a fading heartbeat — its rhythm slowing with every passing moment. Larken knew their old life had ended, severing all ties, releasing all the pain. And now a new life was before them, one that he knew was his choice to live and accept.

On many occasions, Zane had mentioned that he wanted their friendship back. *Just try*, he had pleaded. At the time Larken couldn't, but things had changed now. He wanted their friendship back as well. Caressing Zane's cheek again, he said, "I will try."

Zane knew what Larken meant by that, and his gaze filled with shock and hope...and maybe even love. Yet it wasn't the love Larken used to hope for. Unable to stop himself, Larken leaned in closer.

Then Zane's hand came up to cover his over his cheek. "Larken."

The distress in the vampire's voice had him pausing. He didn't want to hurt anymore. He didn't want Zane to hurt anymore.

But he needed one last kiss goodbye, even if it was just an innocent one. Leaning in the rest of the way, Larken placed a tender kiss on Zane's cheek. A tear fell, following the path of the others, and it was the last one he wanted to cry for this man.

Releasing Zane, he stepped back and looked away. He stood there, silent, staring off into the nothingness that seemed to surround him. He closed his eyes at the feel of Zane's hand brushing against his own. Turning his palm out, he entwined his fingers with Zane's. With his eyes still averted, Larken's heart sank for the last time as the man's hand slowly slipped from his, his chest rising and falling with every heavy breath as Zane left him.

He knew it was a new beginning from here on out — for the both of them. He was scared as hell at what the future might be, but it was one he knew he'd survive, despite how many times he'd thought he'd die of a broken heart. A sense of peace crept its way into him. His heart was his own once again, to live and love as he pleased.

After composing himself, Larken left the library and walked back to the entrance hall. His stomach jumped into his throat as he spotted Zane holding Bo tightly, a blissful look on the dragon's face.

This is how it's meant to be.

He stood frozen as Bo glanced over to him. With one hand gliding up and down Zane's back and the other resting on the back of Zane's head, Bo smiled at Larken and mouthed *thank you.*

The happiness in the dragon's eyes was too much for him, so he looked away. He had wanted that happiness, once, and now he was as confused as ever at what he felt. There was an ache inside him, telling him that something was brewing. There was a heat that burned at his core for something more...something within his grasp...*someone* within his grasp.

Yet he refused to identify it. He couldn't. Not yet. It was too soon.

Chapter Eight

Khale grunted as Ballen stumbled through the castle doors. He was grateful that the vampire had helped him back to the coven, but having his arm over Ballen's shoulders was pulling terribly at his back. Unable to take the pain the awkward position caused, Khale pulled away from Ballen's hold.

"Thanks, Ballen, but I think I can take it from here."

"Are you sure? That was a hard fall you took. If it weren't for the tree branches slowing you down as you fell, I imagine you would've broken quite a few bones."

Khale was pretty sure he would have too, and that wouldn't have been good. Taking days to heal from one broken rib was one thing. Having to heal from several... Well, that'd just be awful.

Placing a gentle hand on Khale's shoulder, Ballen said, "Come on. Let's get you to your room."

As pleasurable as taking a moment to lie down sounded, he knew there wasn't time. Shaking his head, Khale said, "No, we need to get to the war room. We need to tell the others about what happened. The Dráguns might still be nearby, or there could be others. The sooner we tell Remus, the better."

"Don't worry about it. I'll tell them—right after I get you to your room."

He wanted to be there to learn of what Remus planned to do, but Khale figured he'd have someone fill him in on it later. Ballen was right. He needed to get to his room.

On the second floor, though, Khale managed to talk Ballen into leaving him and going to the war room, assuring the vampire that he'd make it the rest of the way to his room just fine—and he did, but it was a slow and painful journey. His whole body ached from the impact of hitting the ground. Various areas of his face stung from the bite of the thinner branches, and some of the cuts were still bleeding.

Heading to his wardrobe, Khale removed his waistcoat and let it fall to the floor—his vest was next and his shirt soon followed after. Opening the wardrobe, he looked into the mirror hanging inside it, observing the thin slashes along his skin and the gouge at the edge of his hairline on his forehead. It didn't look too bad, but though the gouge wasn't bleeding too severely, he knew it'd probably take the rest of the night before it healed completely. Turning around, he looked over his shoulder and inspected his back. Bruises were starting to form but, like Ballen had said, thankfully nothing was broken.

Khale jumped and nearly fell into the wardrobe when his bedroom door crashed open.

"Are you all right?"

Before Khale could answer Larken's question, the vampire was already near him, reaching out to Khale. His first instinct was to back away, to avoid the man's touch, but this time he didn't. He was hurting and craved comfort from another — from Larken.

Khale let out a heavy sigh as Larken framed his face with his hands, his fingertips threading into his hair. He turned his face into the touch, then hissed as a callous on Larken's hand rubbed hard against one of the cuts.

"I'm sorry," Larken said, then he started to pull away.

Quickly reaching up, Khale placed his hands over Larken's, keeping them there. He didn't want to lose the relief he felt from the vampire's touch. "Don't. I don't..." His words failed him as he stared up into Larken's eyes.

Larken smiled, but Khale could still see the concern etched around the corners of his mouth, making Khale want to kiss the worry lines away.

"Dear gods, when Ballen told us what happened..." Larken's brow pulled down, confliction shining in his eyes. "I know you said no before, but... I'm sorry, I..."

Larken's Adam's apple bobbed up and down as the man swallowed, then Khale stood in shock as Larken leaned down and kissed him. Again, his instinct was to pull away, but he couldn't.

He didn't want to.

Moaning, Khale slanted his head as Larken's tongue pushed past his lips and into his mouth, deepening the kiss. The man tasted incredible. He tasted of heat and passion and everything Khale desired. Their tongues fought for dominance, their lips mashing together, seeming to never get enough. Larken fed him groans of lust, spiking Khale's hunger. The vampire's hands traveled along Khale's sides then settled on his ass, squeezing tight and pulling Khale nearer, pressing their hardening cocks together. Of their own accord, Khale's arms came up and wrapped around Larken's neck.

When Larken wound his arms around him, embracing him tightly, Khale gasped and stiffened within his hold.

Jumping back, Larken quickly said, "I'm sorry. I'm so sorry. Did I hurt you?"

Cringing, Khale looked over his shoulder again and assessed the bruises. When he heard the sharp intake of breath, he looked in the mirror to see Larken staring at the reflection of his back.

"Oh, Khale, what's going on?" He moved closer, and this time Khale did back away. "How is it that you have bruises like that?" Larken continued. He looked at Khale's face. "Why aren't you healing? Have you not fed recently? Do you need blood?"

What was he supposed to say to that when he didn't know the answer himself? He'd just fed this evening before he'd joined the others for breakfast, but feeding had never played much part in his healing process. He had a feeling that his inability to heal as quickly as other vampires would never be solved.

Shaking his head, Khale replied, "No, I don't need to feed."

"Are you sure?" Larken reached out for him. "I could—"

Khale backed away more quickly this time. The pain from his back had cleared his head, making him realize that he shouldn't have let Larken touch him before. That he should have ended the kiss immediately. He had his reasons, but he wasn't sure Larken would understand them. "I said no," he said, a little more harshly than he had meant to.

A flash of hurt crossed Larken's features, but his expression quickly turned stoic. His hands dropped to his sides and his lips tightened into a thin line. "All right. I'm sorry to have bothered you." He turned and headed toward the door.

Khale opened his mouth to tell him to stop, to apologize for his tone, but he instead closed it without saying a word and watched Larken exit his room.

* * * *

A few hours later, Larken's head was flying from the double dose of licus he'd taken just moments ago, and he smiled lazily at the ceiling in the library. It seemed only fitting to come back there after Zane and the others had left. This was him trying to let go and this was where he'd done it. Being rejected by Khale — again — struck a nerve inside him. And now he wanted every ounce of *pain* he felt to disappear. He wanted to feel nothing...for no one.

But as he lay there, he couldn't stop the images that slowly began to form high above him. Those beautiful violet eyes shining down at him. That shy smile molded by perfect lips. Larken could hear his voice, the smooth roll of the words as they were spoken. That voice whispered his name, then again with more passion. He wanted to reach out and trace the man's lips, feel the way they shaped and moved under his touch.

"Larken?"

His gaze shot to the end of the couch he lay on. Khale stood there, his gaze so curious and beautiful. Larken couldn't help but smile, a sudden comfort filling him at the sight. Slowly, he got up then placed himself before Khale. He didn't know if it was the licus giving him more confidence than he had, but he reached out and did as he'd fantasized. He brushed his fingers along Khale's mouth.

And it was perfect.

Khale's lips were soft beneath his fingertips. The vampire's mouth parted slightly and Larken ran his thumb along Khale's bottom lip. He wanted to taste what he felt. He wanted to savor the essence of this man in this moment. Their last kiss hadn't been enough. He needed more. Leaning down, he placed his mouth over Khale's, excitement rushing through him from the warmth that seeped into him.

Then suddenly the air was rushing from his lungs as his back hit the wall, pain shooting through his head as it made contact with the hard stone. His vision blurred and he shook his head to clear it.

Blinking hard a few times, he then glared up, ready to question Khale as to why the hell the man had pushed him away. But his chest filled with lead as he watched anger fill Damien's eyes.

"What the fuck, Larken!" Damien wiped his mouth with the sleeve of his shirt.

Larken gaped in shock as the man before him flickered back and forth between looking like Khale then Damien. Larken gave his head a good shake and the image finally settled on his friend. Oh gods, what had he done?

"Damien, I'm so—"

"I don't want to hear it! Fuck, man, what were you thinking? What the hell is wrong with you?"

Larken tried to think of what to say, but the truth was, he didn't know.

Narrowing his eyes, Damien stepped closer, his gaze searching Larken's. His expression turned to one of disappointment and he took a step back. "Dear gods, man, how high are you?"

Larken couldn't even begin to decipher the blur of excuses that ran through his mind.

Sighing, Damien went on, "You know what? It doesn't matter. But I've had enough. I've stood by for too long watching you sulk and pity yourself, and then you go and pull some shit like this. Look, I'm sorry for what's happened to you, but you can't keep doing this. Whatever drug you're taking is going to ruin your life. Seeing as you're my Second Commander, I probably shouldn't be talking to you like this, but as your friend I can't sit by idly and watch you waste away. You're better than this!"

Feeding off Damien's anger, the blood in Larken's veins pumped faster. Who did Damien think he was? "You don't know what I've been through," he gritted out.

"Actually, yes, I do. I've witnessed the whole thing since I've been a part of this coven. I watched you pine over someone that wasn't right for you. And now I've been watching you wallow in a pit of despair because you didn't get what you wanted." Damien quietly cursed and closed his eyes. "Listen, I'm not trying to be mean, but you have to stop this. You have to let go."

Larken's throat constricted. "I have let him go," he breathed out.

"I don't believe you. If you had, then you wouldn't be doing this to yourself."

"Letting go isn't that easy. I need more time!" He did need more time, though that wasn't the reason for his needing the licus in this case—but he didn't want to tell Damien that. He didn't want his friend to know of his rapidly growing feelings for Khale.

"No, you don't!" Damien shot back. "You've had plenty of time. Now it's time to move on, to get over it, and drugging yourself isn't the way to do it." Damien stepped forward and grabbed Larken by the shoulders. "You are the strongest person I know, so I know you can do this. You *have* to." He gave Larken's shoulders a gentle squeeze then backed away. "There's someone else out there for you, my friend, and when you find him, you'll finally be...free. Free to live your life happily. But first you have to let go. And I'm not talking about Zane now. I'm talking about this pain and misery you hold so closely."

After giving Larken a look of concern Damien left him, and Larken couldn't find the words to stop him.

* * * *

Exhausted, Damien walked over and sat on the end of his bed. Rubbing his hands over his face, he thought about what had happened. Larken's behavior had been unsettling at times before, but he hadn't really realized how far gone his friend was until tonight. He only hoped that what he'd said would have some sort of impact and help Larken find his way back.

A knock sounded at his door.

"Come in." Regret at offering admittance filled him as Nikolai entered his room. He was in no mood to have his brain twisted in every other direction right then, and he was sure Nikolai's presence would do just that. The man always did. "What do you want?"

Nikolai crossed the room, a smile playing across his lips. He stopped before Damien and opened his mouth, but no words came out. Instead, his smile slowly faded and a frown spread across his brow.

Damien's breath began to quicken as the Drágun leaned closer to him, their mouths mere inches apart.

He stood still, not knowing what to do as he listened to Nikolai inhale. A chill ran along his spine when Nikolai pulled back, the silver of his irises now a blazing red. Damien had never seen such a thing, and the sight stole his breath. The angry expression and heated gaze never waned as Nikolai stepped back, and it was then that Damien realized what was happening.

Without a word, Nikolai turned on his heel and started toward the door.

Let him go, his conscience urged. *This is what you've wanted – for him to leave you alone.*

But he's got it wrong.

It doesn't matter. Let him leave!

"It's not what you think," he quickly blurted out.

Nikolai looked back to Damien, his lips briefly pulled back in a snarl before he gritted out, "His scent on you suggests otherwise."

When he turned to leave again, Damien's heart jumped in his chest. "It was a mistake." Why? Why was he doing this? Having Nikolai at arm's length was all he'd ever wanted. This simple misunderstanding could give him that. All he had to do was shut up!

But for the life of him, he couldn't.

"It truly isn't what you think," he said again.

With a firm expression on his face, Nikolai closed the door and came back to tower over him. "Is that so? Tell me, then, what was it?"

Having the Drágun this close again had Damien's hackles rising and his own anger began to grow. Why did he feel the need to soothe the man's worries? Nikolai held no claims over him. What happened in his life was none of the Drágun's concern.

"Listen, my business is my own," he spat out. "I don't owe you any explanation."

"Then why did you say anything in the first place?"

What was he supposed to say to that? *Curse this man for getting under my skin!* Glaring up at the Drágun, he shot back, "I don't know!" *Damn it.* Damien wanted to hang his head the moment the words left his mouth. That wasn't what he'd meant to say. Growling, he fisted his hands at his sides. "While it's none of your business, I'll have you know that what happened between me and Larken meant nothing. It was a misunderstanding and was quickly rectified. He and I are just friends — nothing more."

Nikolai's glower began to fade — the wrinkles across his forehead smoothing out and the color of his eyes returning to the magnificent silver that never ceased to captivate Damien.

Nikolai stepped closer, his chest brushing against Damien's. They remained silent for a moment, Damien's heart pounding in his chest as the Drágun stared at him.

"Thank you," Nikolai said softly.

Huffing, Damien looked away. "Like I said, though, it's not like it's any of your business."

Fingers under his chin, forcing him to look back, caught him by surprise. Damien was about to argue the man's audacity, but Nikolai's mouth suddenly over his stopped his words. He tensed as the pressure of Nikolai's lips increased. His mind tried to yell at him, to order him to push the man away, but before he knew it, he was kissing Nikolai back.

This seemed to be all the assurance Nikolai needed. Molding their bodies together, Nikolai cupped his face and deepened the kiss. Melting into the touch, Damien opened his mouth and let Nikolai explore. The taste of him, the heat of his touch, quickly drove Damien to the edge, yet the reality of what was happening came crashing down.

Forcing his hands between them, Damien pushed Nikolai away. *No, I can't do this.*

When Nikolai began to reach for him, Damien shook his head. Swallowing down the lump in his throat, he rasped out, "Leave." Holding his breath, he looked away, unable to witness the pained expression he was sure would be on Nikolai's face.

He stared into the fire blazing in the hearth, listening to Nikolai slowly back away then leave. The moment his door closed the air rushed from his lungs and his knees threatened to give out. Damien stumbled over to a chair and sank down into it then buried his face in his hands.

"Why? Why? *Why!*" He'd been trying so hard to resist Nikolai, why did the bastard have to go and do that? Growling, his scrubbed his hands over his face then ran them through his hair.

It isn't right.

Yes, that was what he'd keep telling himself. Whatever fleeting emotion he might have felt for Nikolai needed to end. *The man is a Drágun for fuck's sake. Zane and Bo may be able to do it, but I can't.*

Is that really the excuse you're going to use?

Damien growled at the unwanted voice butting into his thoughts. He'd use whatever damn excuse he wanted to if it meant not getting hurt. If he didn't open his heart, no one would be able to break it...again.

Chapter Nine

Larken paced back and forth across his room, his anger rising with every muddled thought that ran through his mind.

What Damien had said struck a nerve in him. He didn't care what the man thought about his recreational uses—Larken had his reasons for them.

Sure, what he'd done to Damien was beyond stupid, but he blamed the licus for it. *Well, most of it.*

Larken groaned. He knew why he'd done it. He'd done it because he'd thought that he was kissing Khale. He'd wanted to kiss Khale again and again—and still did. He knew the feeling quickly growing inside him. He recognized it and had felt it before, but it just couldn't be. There was no way he'd let this happen again.

The sound of knocking at his door made his irritation rise. "Go away," he growled. He didn't want to deal with anyone right then. When the knock sounded again, he shouted, "I said go away!" Huffing, he walked over then gripped the back of the couch, his fingers digging in until his knuckles turned white.

When he heard the door to his room open, his anger shot up. "I said…" The last person he'd ever thought would visit him entered his room, unmoved by his shouting.

"Hello, Larken."

"Bo," he acknowledged, narrowing his eyes. "To what do I owe the pleasure?" he added with a bit of sarcasm.

"May I come in?" Not waiting for an answer, Bo joined him in the center of the room.

Glaring at him, Larken asked, "What do you want?"

Bo crossed his arms over his chest and stated, "I know I'm the last person you probably want to talk to, but I feel compelled to ask something on Zane's behalf." The dragon rolled his eyes. "You know Zane. He never confronts anything having to do with emotions."

Larken's patience was beginning to wear thin, and by the look on Bo's face, the dragon was realizing it as well.

"In all honesty," Bo went on, "I don't expect an answer from you, and I probably don't have any right, but I have to ask." He chewed his bottom lip for a moment. "Well, I guess there really is no other way to ask this, so I'll just be frank. What's wrong?"

Larken clenched his hands at his sides. *You're correct, you* don't *have the right.*

Bo gave a short nod. "I can see by your expression that you're not too motivated to answer that."

"You think?"

Sighing, Bo said, "Listen, something…different…is going on with you. Zane sees it. I see it. Everyone sees it. And whether you believe it or not, we all care. I thought seeing as you've known me for the shortest amount of time—so I'm more likely to have the most unbiased opinion—that you'd be more inclined to talk to me." He looked up at Larken with tenderness in his eyes. "I know it'll be hard, but you're holding something in and you need to let it out."

Larken scoffed at the man's assumption. *But it's not an assumption. Why can't I let it out?* Shaking his head, Larken turned his back on him. "You're right. You're the last person I want to talk to."

"Why?"

With that simple question, something cracked inside him. "Because you started all of it! I had everything under control—right on track—and you ruined it!"

Letting out another sigh, Bo pressed his lips together firmly and regarded him. After a moment of silence, he finally asked, "Do you believe in fate?"

Larken's brow furrowed at the question. "No. Why?"

"Because I do. I believe that everything happens for a reason. I go where life—where *fate*—leads me. I may not understand it or always like it, but I deal nonetheless. Fate brought me here, and it was not within my control to change it. I struggled to understand it, but in the end I let go and fate revealed its outcome. I think fate has taken you on this certain path for a reason. You were meant to..." He paused a moment, seeming hesitant. "You were meant to lose him. You were meant to experience heartache."

"Well, ain't that fucking fantastic. I suppose you're going to tell me why."

Bo's face pinched as he scowled. "So you can freely feel for others. Don't you get it? You've done nothing but try to control everything, so much so that you've guarded yourself from all possibilities. Experiencing this heartache has opened up your emotions, left you vulnerable to new things. And they're happening whether you like it or not. New things have entered your life and it scares you. It scares you that you feel again."

But it's too soon! Yes, I want Khale, but I can't love him – not yet. "Life has to have balance," Larken shot back. "Therefore there has to be control."

"But not over everything. There are some things fate guides you with."

"Like what?"

Bo leaned forward and pierced him with a fierce gaze. "Answer me honestly. If you had never fallen in love with Zane, if your heart had been free from the beginning, would you have even given Khale a second glance?"

Larken stiffened at the sound of Khale's name. "What are you talking about?"

Waving a hand through the air dismissively, Bo said, "Don't worry. I don't think too many people see what's going on between the two of you, but something *is* going on. The look you two shared when he first arrived here said it all. Now, I ask again, under other circumstances, would you have given Khale a second glance?"

Larken wanted to bury his face in his hands. *Oh gods, how many other people have noticed?*

"Larken?"

Throwing his hands in the air, Larken shouted, "I wouldn't have, all right? The kid is bossy and arrogant and thinks he's above all others!" Larken began pacing the room again. "He drives me fucking crazy." *His mouth is what drives me crazy.*

"All right, so you admit you would have paid him no heed, but that's not how things turned out. You *did* fall in love with Zane. You *did* get your heart broken, forcing you to let go of your emotions. And with that, you managed to find love again."

"No! You don't know what you're talking about," Larken snarled. "I cannot love him. It's too soon."

"Why?" That one word came out more as a plea than a question.

"Because I'm still in love with Zane!" Larken sucked in a sharp breath. He hadn't meant to say that out loud because it wasn't true, but it was what he'd been used to saying in the past. He *had* finally let Zane go, but he still held the man too closely. He knew it was his fear of what he was feeling for Khale that made him still hold onto what he had felt for Zane. He knew that everything Damien had said was true, and that pissed him off even more.

He glanced over to Bo—the dragon's eyes were wide at Larken's admission.

"Are you?" Bo asked softly.

No. Yes. No! Dear gods, I'm so confused! No, I don't love Zane. And no, I can't love Khale. It's. Too. Soon.

Bo looked at him questioningly. "Why did you let him go then?"

Larken's anger surged through him. "Because of you! It'll always be you! It's you he wanted. It's you he loves. And in the end, it's *you* he chose. And I hate that." He gritted his teeth together and ground out, "I hate you."

Larken regretted the words the moment they had left him, and seeing the stricken expression on Bo's face ate at him even more. He wanted to apologize— he *should* apologize—but when he opened his mouth to speak, he failed to form the words.

Bo's gaze flitted across the room as he clearly tried to compose himself. "I see." With his chest rising and falling with heavy breaths, Bo nodded and said, "I guess I should go then. I'm sorry to have bothered you."

Larken's chest tightened as he watched Bo exit his room. He couldn't take it. He didn't want to deal with the pain and emotions that filled him.

Stomping across the room, he snatched up the wooden box that held the licus and opened it. "No!" Larken clawed at the empty case as if his touch would magically make more leaves appear. Roaring, he threw the box across the room, taking little satisfaction in watching it splinter and break into pieces. Desperate, he ripped open the doors of his desk in search of more.

Larken's body stiffened with every second that ticked by. The confrontation with Bo had diminished the effects of the licus he'd taken earlier. He needed more. He needed his release. He was tired of being so angry all of the time.

But who am I angry with? Bo? Zane? Khale? Why is this feeling driving me crazy, and why am I letting it?

Larken shook his head — he knew the answer, and he didn't like it. Whether he'd accepted it or not, he knew that he was only angry with himself — and he was taking it out on everyone else.

He violently sifted through the cupboards of his desk, but when he came up empty-handed he snapped. Raking his arm across the top surface, Larken sent everything there tumbling to the floor.

When he felt a hand on his shoulder, Larken spun around and captured the intruder by the throat.

Khale's eyes widened as he grasped at Larken's hand. "Larken," he sputtered out. "It's just me."

With his anger barely ebbing, Larken loosened his hold. "What are *you* doing here?"

Khale fought against him. "I knocked, but you didn't hear. When I heard the crash... Damn it, Larken, let go!"

Seeing the fierceness in Khale's eyes had Larken losing what little bit of control he had left. He just couldn't hold back anymore.

He slid his hand around to the back of Khale's neck and pulled him forward, crushing their mouths together. He'd tried before, tried luring the vampire to him, and Khale had turned him away. Larken knew Khale was fighting *something* when it came to him, always dodging him. The few times they'd been together had been proof enough that Khale wanted him as well. Larken wasn't going to let go, not this time. He wrapped his free arm around Khale and pressed their bodies together. Khale briefly stiffened under his hold, but soon melted into his touch.

Grinding against each other, Larken backed Khale up until the man bumped into the back of the couch. Releasing his lips, Larken trailed hurried kisses along Khale's throat. He attacked the buttons of Khale's waistcoat, but with fumbling fingers he gave up and ripped the thing open—its remaining buttons scattering across the floor. Sliding the garment off Khale's shoulders, he then quickly untucked the man's shirt and pushed it up and over his head. Wasting no more time, he leaned down and latched onto one of Khale's nipples.

Khale cried out and arched into his touch. "Oh gods, Larken." He took several deep breaths. "I... I can't be doing this."

Larken growled. *Not this again.*

Kneeling, he nipped at Khale's side. "Then tell me *no*," he ground out as he nibbled his way down Khale's side. While running his hands around to

Khale's back and pressing his chest against the man's hard cock, he bit hard at the spot just above Khale's hip bone.

Letting out a deep groan, Khale took hold of Larken's hair, holding him in place. "Yes," he hissed.

That was all Larken needed. He'd gone too long without being inside Khale, and he craved it more than anything he'd craved before.

Spinning Khale around, Larken took hold of his hands and put them on the back of the couch. "Hold on and don't move," he ordered.

Khale did as he was told, and Larken felt a new spark of desire flood him. Reaching around, he untied Khale's pants then yanked them down. Stripping off his own shirt, Larken then opened his pants and pulled his cock free. He stroked himself as he watched Khale's back flex as the man breathed deeply, noting that the bruises had all but faded. Dropping to his knees once again, Larken spread Khale's cheeks and dove in, lapping at the inviting hole before him. He forced his tongue inside the tight channel, delighting in the feel of the ring of muscle clenching down around his tongue. Khale cried out again and pressed his ass harder against Larken's face.

Damn kid never learns.

Growling, Larken pulled away, only to then bite down on Khale's right butt cheek. Then without warning, Larken shoved two fingers into Khale's hole. Khale sucked in a deep breath, his hips jerking forward then back, forcing Larken's fingers to go deeper. "I said don't move," Larken spoke roughly as he started to fuck Khale with his fingers.

Khale hung his head and trembled. "I... I..." He gasped again. "Oh gods, please don't stop."

A satisfying grin crept over Larken's face. He loved seeing Khale bend to his will. He slowly stood, all the while continuing the invasion with his fingers — adding a third as he rose up. He nuzzled behind Khale's ear. "If you don't hold still, I *am* going to stop."

Khale shuddered. "No, don't stop," he begged.

Larken licked along the side of his throat. "Then hold still," he crooned.

Nodding, Khale breathed out, "Yes."

Larken smiled and pushed his fingers in deeply, then pulled them out, hearing Khale whimper. Slowly, he walked backward across the room, not wanting to miss a single moment of the beautiful sight — Khale's legs spread as wide as the pants around his ankles allowed, his body shuddering with pleasure. Larken grabbed the bottle of oil off his bedside table then quickly returned. He loved seeing Khale that way, but he didn't at the same time. He didn't want to see Khale suffering with need. Larken needed to give the man everything he wanted. And at that moment, anything Khale asked of him, Larken knew he would give it.

Oiling up his straining erection, Larken then pressed against Khale's opening. Leaning forward, Larken wound his arms around Khale then brought his hands up to clamp down over the man's shoulders. When the head of Larken's cock breached his entrance, Khale quivered against him.

Gods, how he loved the feel of this man.

Digging his fingers into Khale's muscles, Larken entered the rest of the way in one quick thrust.

Khale sucked in a deep breath, his body stiffening. For a brief moment Larken feared he'd hurt him, but when he felt Khale push his ass back slightly, his worries fled. Sliding his hands down to Khale's waist, he pressed his chest to the man's back and whispered, "I'm going to fuck you now."

"Oh gods, yes!"

Even if he'd wanted to, Larken wouldn't have been able to hold back. He pounded into the tight heat that engulfed his cock, his pace fast and hard. Putting one hand between Khale's shoulders, he pressed down until Khale was bent over, his chest brushing the top of the couch. With his other hand, he reached down and grabbed Khale's braid. Taking hold of the end of it, he rolled his wrist, wrapping half of the braid around his hand.

A new hunger filled him as Khale's head tilted back when he tugged at the man's hair. Larken's deep growl reverberated throughout the room, the noise mixing with the sound of skin slapping against skin as Larken's hips barreled back and forth. He pressed down on the middle of Khale's back, forcing him to arch, his ass tilting up higher, allowing Larken to slide in deeper.

Khale's grunts with every deep thrust were like music to his ears, the divine sound sending a shiver through him. A familiar tingle formed at the base of his spine, his balls tightening and ready for release.

Tugging on the man's braid, he urged Khale to stand up. Khale moaned at the new angle and ground his ass back more, his hips swiveling. That was nearly Larken's undoing.

With his one hand still firmly wrapped in Khale's hair, Larken reached around and splayed his other hand over Khale's chest. Licking along the curve of his neck, he whispered, "Come for me." Then, giving into another desire of his, Larken sank his teeth into the warm flesh, relishing the taste of Khale's essence as it poured into his mouth.

Khale shouted and his hole tightened around Larken's cock. Looking down, Larken watched as ropes of cum painted the back of his couch.

Now that... *That* was his undoing. Giving Khale a pleasure so intimate, so rapturous, was all he needed to find his own release.

Panting, Khale rested his head back against Larken's shoulder as Larken licked the small puncture wounds closed. He gently unwound his hand from the man's braid then lightly massaged the base of Khale's head.

Placing tender kisses along his throat, Larken asked, "I didn't hurt you, did I?"

Khale rolled his head back and forth on his shoulder. "Uh-uh."

Larken grinned against the soft skin. "Good." He hugged Khale closer to him, his now flaccid cock slipping from Khale's channel. His eyelids soon became heavy as exhaustion overcame him. After removing the few clothes they still had on, he took Khale's hand and guided him to his bed. They crawled in under the blankets then settled into each other's arms.

Not once had he ever brought a man to his bed to sleep, to hold each other as they drifted off into a deep slumber, yet with Khale, it felt right.

Holding Khale at that moment had him seeing clearly. He was tired of being so angry all of the time. He knew that Damien was right. He'd held onto his sadness and hurt for too long. It was time to let go. And Bo, to whom he seriously still needed to apologize, was right as well. It was hard for him to believe, but he knew he could feel for someone else again, and he'd found that with Khale.

It was all happening so fast, but he somehow knew that this was what he wanted. He wanted Khale. He wanted Khale for more than just sex. He realized that the burning desire in him was more than just a physical reaction—it was hidden feelings of love and wanting.

Larken wasn't sure what he was supposed to do next, but he hoped that when he woke he and Khale could figure it out together.

Khale listened as Larken's breathing evened out, and he knew the man had fallen asleep. Rolling over within Larken's hold, Khale stared at him, taking in the vampire's peaceful features as he slept soundly. His heart beat harder in his chest as he replayed the intimacy they'd just shared. He hadn't known that that was going to happen. Seeing the hurt on the vampire's face earlier, Khale felt drawn to comfort him, even though he knew he probably shouldn't. When Larken had walked away, Khale hadn't followed. Despite what he had felt, he knew he had to try to stay away. But as the hours had passed he hadn't been able to take it. He'd needed to see if Larken was all right. He'd never thought his coming to Larken's room would lead to...

Khale closed his eyes and sighed deeply. What they'd shared had been incredible, and he felt his resolve to obey his father slip away. He didn't know what it was about Larken, but he needed him, craved him—was drawn to him with a force so powerful that he didn't know if he could hold back.

But he had to. What they shared could go nowhere. Once he had finished gathering information on the coven and its warriors, he would have to return home. Within the few days he'd been here, it had become clear to him that Keddrick and his men were doing no wrong. They cared for their people and each other, and Khale could see that they were doing everything they could to find Gravaick. So he knew he'd probably be returning to his father with nothing that would help the man. He knew what Vardel was trying to do, and he knew it wouldn't work.

But still, he'd give it a week. If he returned home too soon, he was sure his father would be angry, saying that he hadn't given it enough time. Until then, he had to try to avoid Larken as much as he could. There was no point in serving up his heart only to have it broken. Surprisingly, he didn't care anymore about what his father would say. Maybe it was being in Larken's arms that had given him strength, but for the first time he felt like his own man, that *all* of his decisions were his to make. He loved what he and Larken shared, and he couldn't believe he'd denied himself these pleasures for so long. Maybe it was also being away from his father—being on his own, seeing that there were others out there who cared—that had made him realize that he didn't need to hold his longing for his father's acceptance so closely. He wanted to be loved, and wanted to love in return, and he hoped one day he could find it. But he knew he couldn't— shouldn't—find it with Larken. Larken was a warrior, and Khale was a guard of his city. Allengard was where he was needed, and Larken was needed here.

They could never have a future, and he needed to accept that.

"I don't want to, but I have to distance myself from you," he whispered as he lightly brushed his fingers over Larken's cheek. "It's the only way that'll make leaving you easier." Khale had fallen hard and fast for the warrior, and he hated that he'd have to give him up.

Chapter Ten

A week had passed with no new mystery for Khale to find. As he'd suspected, Keddrick and his men seemed to be doing everything they could to help their people. They'd even been kind enough to allow Khale to join in on their meetings, despite his low ranking. So here he sat, quietly by the hearth, half listening as the men went over strategies and possible places Gravaick could be hiding.

"I have a question," Wesley said.

Khale had found it kind of odd that the human mate was allowed there seeing as he wasn't even a warrior, but usually the man just doted over Remus and kept quiet. To hear him speak up drew Khale's attention.

"Yes, Wesley," Keddrick replied.

The human furrowed his brow as he sat back in his chair. "Well, when you find Gravaick, what is it that you plan on doing? I mean, how are you going to fight him?"

"What do you mean?" The sire looked at him confused—mirroring Khale's own bewilderment at the question. "We will fight him as we always do."

"See, but that's just it," Wesley said. "You always fight the same. And, I'm sorry if I'm speaking out of place here, but that hasn't worked so well for you in the past."

"*Wesley*," Remus chided.

"No, no"—Keddrick raised his hand, cutting his commander off—"I want to hear this." He leaned forward, a stern gaze in his eyes. "Do you have a better idea, Wesley? Something we warriors haven't thought of in the past centuries?"

Khale could see the reluctance in the human's expression, but the little man also seemed determined to speak his mind.

Wesley glanced hesitantly in Khale's direction before he said, "It's not necessarily a better idea per se, but it is one that I know you've thought of before."

Keddrick's intense gaze turned into a glare. "No."

"Oh come on. You know it will take care of everything."

Khale sat forward in his chair, eagerly wanting to know what the two men were talking about.

"I said no."

"But why?" Wesley all but whined.

Keddrick stood abruptly, towering over the smaller man, making Wesley shrink back in his chair. But to Khale's surprise, Wesley didn't give up.

"You know deep down that it'll work," the human went on. "Get the *piloats* back from Barend, take the trip to—"

"No!" Keddrick pounded his fist onto the tabletop.

What's a piloats? Trip to where?

Remus placed his hand on Wesley's arm. "That's enough."

Shaking his head, Wesley sat up straight in his chair again and looked to his mate. "But this isn't fair. You

know you can beat him if you just give it a chance."
He turned his attention back to the sire. "Please. It
only has to be a one-time thing. You can send them
back as soon as it's over."

Send what back? Khale's gaze shot back and forth
between the two men, trying his hardest to figure out
what the hell they were talking about.

"It's too dangerous, I told you that. If Gravaick got
his hands on any of it during the fight—"

"He wouldn't know what to do with it!" Wesley cut
in.

"He's not stupid," Keddrick barked out. "It
wouldn't take him long to figure it out—especially if
he watched what we were doing." He shook his head.
"No, it's too dangerous. I won't bring that kind of
destruction to my world. End of discussion!" Keddrick
took a deep breath and sat back down. "Besides"—he
glanced over to Nikolai—"I'm kind of hoping we'll
have a greater weapon on our side when the time
comes."

Khale watched as Nikolai's features hardened. "You
mean the mages, right?" the Drágun gritted out.

Keddrick sneered and replied dryly, "Yeah, that."

The room fell silent and Khale's head swam with the
hundreds of questions he had, but he figured he
wouldn't get any answers if he asked. The men skirted
around the specifics of whatever they were talking
about, and Khale was pretty sure it was because he
was in the room.

He had a feeling that he'd finally come across
something his father would want to hear about, but
whatever they spoke of clearly wouldn't be good for
them. Khale found himself questioning his curiosity,
but he knew in his heart that Keddrick only wanted
what was best.

Maybe he'd try to do a little digging later, see if he could find out what this *piloats* was and what it was used for.

"I think we're done for the night." Keddrick sighed and rubbed his forehead. "We'll continue this after the celebration of the new year."

"We are still celebrating in Diidlon?" Larken asked.

Khale's breath caught at the sound of his voice. They'd barely spoken the entire week. The vampire hadn't seemed too pleased with him, and Khale didn't blame him. He was pretty sure that Larken hadn't been too happy to wake up alone that last night they'd been together. Khale had wanted to stay, to bask in the warmth and pleasure that he'd felt in Larken's arms, but he knew it'd be harder to walk away in the end, and he *had* to walk away.

Maybe he should apologize. What he'd done hadn't been nice, and it would only be right to settle things between them. He didn't want to spend the rest of his time here avoiding Larken. While he couldn't have Larken in the way he wanted, he still wanted them to be civil, to converse and get along. Yes, that's what he'd do. First chance he got, he'd apologize to Larken.

Khale cleared his thoughts and brought his attention back to the others.

"Yes, Larken, we're still going to Diidlon," Keddrick answered. "We've gone to that village to celebrate every year and I don't think we should change that. Although our time should be spent on our search, our people need this. I fear their hopes are diminishing and I think it'll be good to go there and show them we're still here for them, that we care and will do whatever it takes to bring this damn war to an end." He looked to Remus. "I don't want the coven to be left completely empty, though, so have at least ten men stay behind to protect it."

"I agree," Remus added.

"Then it's settled." Keddrick stood then headed for the door. "Have everyone take the rest of the night off and tell them we'll leave at nightfall tomorrow."

* * * *

Gravaick rubbed his chin as he waited for the men to gather around. Knowing that it was past time that he make a move on the vampires, he had spent the day thinking of what action to take. As the cold of the winter air filled the corners of the cave, it reminded him of how quickly the year had gone by and that a new one was upon them. And as that chill crept into his bones, he thought of the celebrations that would be going on.

His people celebrated more than any species he knew of. Maybe it was to celebrate the possibilities a new year brought, and maybe it was to celebrate another year that they'd survived. Either way, his men wouldn't be joining in the usual gatherings that took place in Hollon. He wasn't quite ready to put his men out there so openly, to allow them to drink their stresses away, leaving them vulnerable to any attacks.

It was that that had him thinking of the vampire warriors. He knew their traditions. He knew the tiny village they went to on the eve before every new year, and he wondered if they'd be so careless as to go there this year. It was something the vampires had always done, never missing a year even since the war began, but now it was different. Now it was getting closer to the end. He could feel it. The rule of the vampires was coming to an end, and he was ready to take their place. He could feel in his gut that their morale was slipping, and he knew just the way to slice at it even more.

"Everybody, listen up," he ordered as the last few Dráguns gathered near. "We've been hiding away in this godsforsaken cave for too long, and I'm ready to let some of you out to play." This caught his men's attention and he was happy to see their interest in something other than sitting around doing nothing. "I'm hoping that the vampire warriors are stupid enough to go to Diidlon to welcome the new year, and when they get there, we are going to have a surprise waiting for them. Diidlon is a small village, housing mere farmers and peasants, people weak enough that a handful of you can take care of. And this is what you're going to do. We need to show Keddrick and his men that we're still here and that we don't plan on giving up. So your orders are simple. You will go to Diidlon and destroy it. I want every last man, woman and child slain. I want their cries for help echoing in the air, the blood still pouring out of them as the warriors arrive."

"My lord, the only way that'll happen is if we wait till just before they get there."

"Yes, Flagos, that is correct—very observant of you." *Fucking idiot.*

"But, my lord, wouldn't that risk the chance of us being caught by them?"

The urge to kill his second in command for pure stupidity was growing stronger by the day. "I suggest you run fast then," he snarled. "At daybreak, twenty of you will head out, and not a single one of you had better return before your task is complete."

* * * *

Larken sat back on his couch with a sigh, but before he could get comfortable, someone was knocking at his door. He pinched the bridge of his nose as he got up to see who it was. His headaches were becoming worse, and he knew it was his body punishing him for denying it the licus it craved. After that night when he'd kissed Damien and practically attacked Khale, he'd told himself that enough was enough. The drug was taking control of him and he couldn't let that happen. He needed to be strong and steadfast, and he knew he couldn't do that if he continued to abuse his body with potencies that impaired his judgment.

Opening the door, he was surprised to see Khale standing on the other side. His body immediately took notice of the young man, but Larken forced his desires aside. As much as he wanted Khale, it was apparent that the vampire didn't feel the same. Larken had got that message loud and clear when he'd woken up alone. Khale had been avoiding him since. He rarely ate meals with the rest of them. He requested tasks that were always away from Larken and during their nightly meetings with Keddrick, Khale never spoke to him if he didn't have to—so Larken was a little surprised that the man was there with him now.

"May I come in?" Khale asked politely.

The sweet tone of his voice had Larken's mouth rapidly going dry with desire. Unable to form words, he simply nodded and stepped back to give Khale room to pass. His heart beat harder as he caught a faint whiff of the man's scent. Truly he had never thought he could fall for another after Zane, but having Khale close to him now sent a feeling through him that warmed him from the inside out. It wasn't just his body that wanted Khale. It was his heart.

He only wished that Khale could feel the same. Larken seemed doomed yet again to love a man who wouldn't love him back.

What's wrong with me?

As Larken closed the door, he noticed Khale fidgeting with his hands as his gaze darted around the room.

Why does he look nervous?

"What can I do for you?" Larken asked. He kept his hands fisted at his sides as he passed Khale, too afraid he'd reach out for him. Making his way back to the couch, he then sat down and waited for Khale's response. Larken felt as if the air was being sucked from the room when the young man followed suit and sat down next to him. It had been hard enough seeing Khale around the castle and not going to him— touching him, kissing him, caressing and making love to him—and having him this close now made it incredibly hard for Larken to resist.

Khale shifted a bit then finally looked at him. "I… I wanted to say sorry about…"

Larken knew what Khale was trying to say and his heart fluttered at the sorrow in Khale's voice. He could tell that the vampire felt bad, and he hoped that meant that Khale was ready to reconcile whatever it was that had caused the distance between them.

"Yes?"

Khale's brow furrowed as he caught his bottom lip between his teeth. "About that night, last week…uh… I shouldn't have left the way I did and I'm sorry. I want… I…"

Larken scooted closer, his knee lightly brushing against Khale's. "What?" he asked softly. "What do you want?"

Say it. Say you want me. Please. I know I sound like a desperate fool — even if only to myself — but I need this... I need you.

Closing his eyes, Khale took a deep breath then let it out slowly. "Look, I'm sorry for the other night. I'm sorry I allowed things to go as far as they did." His gaze shot up to meet Larken's. "I mean, I'm not saying I didn't enjoy it, but I should have stopped it. I shouldn't have said yes."

What little bit of hope Larken had disappeared. Relaxing back against the couch, he let out a tired sigh and stared at the fire burning in the hearth. "So we're back to this again."

Sounding defensive, Khale asked, "What's that supposed to mean?"

"You keep saying that we shouldn't be doing what we've done, yet it's clear to see that you want it." Larken glared at him. "So why? Why are you holding back?"

It was Khale's turn to gaze at the fire. Minutes passed by before Khale replied, "I don't know what to tell you. There are many reasons why being together is a bad idea."

"All I need is one."

Khale shook his head and closed his eyes. "I'm sure you'd find a way to talk me out of any of them."

"Well then, there you go." Larken threw his hands up, frustrated with Khale's evasiveness. "If I'd be able to talk you out of them so easily, then they obviously aren't good enough reasons."

Khale looked over to him, his eyes narrowed and lips pursed. "You don't know anything about me, so how would you know whether or not my reasons are good enough?" He shook his head and waved Larken off when he went to respond. "One way or another, I can't have what I want, so there's no point in going after it."

"So you *do* want me?"

Khale seemed surprised that he'd let that slip. "I'm… I'm not saying that," he sputtered.

Larken arched an eyebrow and looked at him, amused. "I think you do."

"Argh!" Jumping up off the couch, Khale glared down at him. "Why do you always have to be so presumptuous?"

"I'm not," he shot back. "You said it, not me."

"Well, forget what I said." The vampire let out a frustrated growl. "You know what? I came here to apologize—"

"And to say 'it can never happen again'," Larken cut in sarcastically.

"Yes, that too! So, I've said my piece, and now I'm going to go."

Khale began to stomp his way toward the door, but Larken ran over and stopped him. Khale's chest brushed against his as the man huffed, and Larken's body tightened from the touch. He could see the irritation in Khale's eyes, but he could also see the longing—the wanting hidden so deep below. Ignoring Khale's requests, he leaned in and kissed him. It was gentle, tender, and oh so heartwarming. He sensed the tension radiating from Khale, but it pleased him that the man didn't pull away. Larken moved his lips slowly, savoring the feel, then reluctantly ended it. He didn't want Khale to feel his space was being invaded, so he backed up and gave Khale room to leave if he wanted.

Khale's breath seemed even more ragged then. He licked his lips as he looked up at Larken. "P-please." He swallowed hard. "Please, don't do that again."

But Larken wanted to, and even watching Khale walk away now, he knew that Khale did too.

* * * *

The Dráguns had invaded Diidlon, and Sove could barely stomach the sight around him.

He held his breath as he watched Callex pin the young vampire down on the ground. The man struggled against Callex's hold as the Drágun unsheathed his dagger. He brought the weapon to the vampire's throat and Sove had to look away. His insides turned at the sound of gurgled blood. Slowly, he looked back just as Callex sat on his haunches, the Drágun's hand firmly planted on the vampire's chest, holding him down as the he fought for breath.

Callex turned to him and smiled. "Come here."

Keeping a steady expression, Sove walked over to stand next to him.

Releasing his hold on the vampire and standing up, Callex pointed to the torch in Sove's hand and said, "Burn him."

Sove's breath caught once again. He looked down at the vampire slowly bleeding to death, then to the torch he held. *Burn him?* Dear gods, he didn't think he could do that. Burning down the village he'd been able to do. But this?

"Do it!" Callex ordered.

Sove's hands shook as he stared down at the vampire.

"Oh, for fuck's sake!" Callex ripped the torch from his hand and pressed it against the young man's chest.

Swallowing down the bile that threatened to erupt from his stomach, he watched in horror as the vampire thrashed around until he finally lay limp.

Callex shoved the torch back in Sove's hand and spat out, "You're so weak."

Sove let out a shuddering breath as Callex walked away, then traveled his gaze over the damage he and the others had done.

Their orders had been to burn the people of the village alive, to have their screams filling the night. But once afire, the vampires had kept rolling around in the snow to put out the flames. Sove recalled it had gotten personal when Flagos had issued new orders. "Slit their throats before you burn them," he'd said, making it harder for them to fight for their lives. Yet Sove still couldn't do it, he couldn't take an innocent life.

He and a few others had long ago decided that they no longer believed in Gravaick. The Drágun had proven to be nothing but a madman on a ludicrous quest to destroy the vampires. They had wanted to leave, but knew Gravaick would kill them for their 'treachery'. So for years they'd hid on the sidelines, making it appear as if they believed in and followed Gravaick's rule.

As for tonight, they went about burning the homes—it was the only thing they could do to not stand out.

He coughed as a wave of smoke blew around him. There was nothing left. Not a single vampire remained standing. The men and women, even the children—all were dead.

"They're coming!" Voren hollered as he ran through the town. He stopped before Flagos, panting for air. "They're coming, the warriors. They're almost here."

Flagos nodded then looked around to the others. "Fall back to the trees," he ordered.

They did as they were told, but Sove didn't understand. "Why aren't we leaving?"

Flagos gave him a sideways glance. "Because we're waiting," he replied.

Still confused, he asked, "For what?"

A menacing expression crossed the Drágun's features. "I'm tired of this shit," Flagos growled out. "It's ridiculous that we do all of this just to walk away. Not this time." He removed an arrow from his quiver. "This ends tonight."

Sove's eyes widened as he realized what Flagos was doing. "Are you fucking kidding me? You're going to get us all killed. There's bound to be at least twice as many of them as there are us."

"Ye of little faith," Flagos snarled. "I'm in charge now, and I said it ends tonight! Now, go tell the others. Tell them to wait for my signal."

Sove clenched his hands at his sides. "And what signal will that be?"

A coy grin spread over Flagos' face. "When I let loose the first arrow, sending Keddrick to his knees."

A knot formed in the pit of his stomach, but he did as he was told. Gathering the men together, he relayed Flagos' orders. He wasn't surprised to see most of the men smiling, happy that they would get to fight, but a few like Sove remained silent. As casually as he could, he wondered over to Wallace.

"I don't like this," Wallace whispered as soon as Sove was in front of him.

"I agree."

Wallace looked past him to the village beyond, a glimmer of worry flashing in his eyes. Looking back to Sove he slightly shook his head. "I can't do this."

"Again, I agree." Sove wished that Nikolai were still with them. He'd always known what to do in situations like this.

Sove ground his teeth as he contemplated his thoughts. He knew that there were twelve Dráguns ready to fight, and eight that felt the same as him and Wallace. There *was* something they could do about this, but he didn't know if it would work out for them in the end. "Listen, I have an idea."

"What is it?"

He stared Wallace in the eyes. "It's simple. We won't fight."

Wallace's gaze widened. "What?"

Looking over his shoulder to the others that were preparing for battle, he said, "Let them get themselves killed. Fighting the vampires is what they want, so let them have it." He turned back to Wallace. "They're bound to be outnumbered, so let the vampires take them down. Once it's done, we can return to Gravaick and tell him that we managed to get away."

Wallace frowned. "And what if some live? What if they actually defeat the vampires?"

Shaking his head, Sove replied, "They won't defeat them. Even if Flagos does manage to get Keddrick down on the first shot, the other vampires are just as strong and capable of taking us all down."

"And if some of them live and run back to Gravaick?"

Dread filled him as he thought of that possibility. "Then I'll take care of it. I'll figure something out."

He could tell that Wallace was hesitant about the idea, but his friend finally nodded in agreement. "All right."

"Good. Now help me tell the others. Start with Stalo, but be careful you're not overheard."

Giving one last short nod, Wallace walked away.

Taking a deep breath, Sove closed his eyes and prayed that this night would end in their favor.

Chapter Eleven

Khale kept his back straight as he rode along with the others. Hearing a few of them whisper about still not wanting him and his men there bit at his nerves, but there was no way he would let them see it. He knew that they spoke just loudly enough for him to hear, that they did it just to piss him off—and it was working. *But what right do they have?* "They're just as new to the coven as I am," he grumbled to himself.

"He isn't even a true warrior," Corben whispered. "Having his daddy get him in is bullshit."

All of a sudden Larken was riding next to them. "Gentlemen," he said firmly. "I'm sure you have more intelligent things to discuss, yes? Better yet, how about you just shut up altogether?" His tone held a seriousness that left no room for argument and the young men ducked their heads in shame. "Good." Larken then looked back to him. "A word, please."

Khale was hesitant, but he followed Larken and guided his horse off the path where they stopped and remained silent as the others passed them.

Once alone, Larken turned to him. "Don't listen to those idiots."

Arching an eyebrow, Khale replied, "Are you serious? Please, do not have this discussion with me. I am not a child that needs reassurance." Khale rolled his eyes then looked away. "I can't believe we're even talking about this."

With a hand under Khale's chin, Larken forced Khale to look back at him. "Don't get so pissy." He released his hold and settled back on his mare. "It just shows that you are letting them get to you."

Glaring, Khale directed his horse around so that he could face Larken head on. "I can take care of myself. There isn't anything they can say that I can't handle."

Larken shook his head. "My gods, you're a stubborn kid." The corners of his mouth then edged up and he grinned. "You are quite adorable, though, when you get all uptight like this."

"Fucking hell, Larken, not this again."

With a gleam in his eye, Larken nudged his horse forward a few steps—his leg now brushing against Khale's. His smile grew as he leaned in. "Tell me to back away then."

Khale's heartbeat skipped at Larken's closeness, then the man's lips were pressed against his. He wanted to pull back, to turn away and keep his heart from falling any further than it already had, but instead he leaned into him, opening his mouth to Larken's probing tongue. He forced his hands to remain still, to not reach up and cup the vampire's face. He wanted to feel the roughness of the man's stubble along his palms. He wanted to feel the silkiness of his hair as he ran his fingers through it. He wanted to tilt his head to the side and deepen the kiss as much as possible, but he didn't. He simply moved his mouth in time with

Larken's, reveling in the illicit moment. The taste of Larken's lips and the touch of his tongue were divine.

Larken nibbled along Khale's bottom lip then pulled away.

With his eyes still closed, Khale tried to savor the essence Larken left behind. He let out a low groan, his cock now aching painfully. "You really have to stop doing that," Khale mumbled, but his heart was screaming for the vampire to lean in and kiss him again.

Larken graced him with a chaste, playful kiss, then said, "One day you will give in, Khale, and I'll be waiting for you. Now come on. We mustn't fall too far behind." With one last coy grin, he nudged his heels into his horse's sides and left Khale staring at the trees.

Closing his eyes again, Khale took in a deep breath then let it out slowly. Once in control of his body, he guided his horse to catch up with the others. Yet when he got there, every good feeling he had vanished.

He stared in shock at the burning village before him. "My gods," he breathed out. When there should have been the sounds of joyful music filling the air, there was instead the roaring of flames that ate at the homes. Red soaked the snow every which way he looked and where bodies strewn along the ground. Khale dismounted then made his way to where Keddrick stood over a fallen vampire. He could see that the woman had once been very lovely, but her deathly pale skin and the blood that covered her stole that beauty away. Even without investigating the village, he knew that there would be no survivors. Innocent lives had been taken...his fellow vampires slaughtered.

There was only one person who would do such a thing, and Khale vowed to himself then that he would do whatever it took to help bring Gravaick down.

Kneeling down, Keddrick brushed the woman's bloody hair from her face, then with his fingertips he closed her eyes. He cupped her cheek and whispered a few parting words. When he rose again, his bloody hands hung loosely at his sides.

Remorse was heavy in the air as they all stood in silence. Damien walked up to stand by Keddrick and he placed a comforting hand on his shoulder. "Sire —" With a sharp intake of breath, his words abruptly ended.

The world around them seemed to still as Damien staggered back, an arrow buried deep in his chest — in his heart.

Larken watched in horror as Damien began to fall. Rushing forward, he caught his friend before he hit the ground. Chaos broke out around him as Dráguns quickly appeared, flanking them from the woods to the north and south of them. The sudden eruption of battle rattled him, but Larken couldn't seem to draw his focus away from the man in his arms.

Damien gasped for air as blood poured out of his mouth. He thrashed around in Larken's hold and tried to remove the arrow.

"No." Larken moved Damien's hand away. "If you take that out, you'll bleed out in seconds." With a shaking hand, he caressed his friend's cheek, trying to soothe him. His senses escaped him as he tried to think of what to do.

A loud clash just above his head had him falling back in shock. Larken looked up and his breath caught at the sight of Khale's sword holding off that of a

Drágun. With swift movements, Khale unsheathed his dagger and buried it in the Drágun's chest. Realization that he'd almost lost his head brought him back to the present and he knew he had to move quickly.

"I need you to protect us, Khale. Follow me." He lifted Damien in his arms and hurried him into the woods and away from the others. Laying his friend down gently in the snow, Larken then removed the cloak from around his neck. He knew that the arrow needed to come out, but he also knew that Damien would need to take in just as much blood as he'd be losing if he wanted to stay alive.

"You saved my life once, my friend, and now it is my turn to do the same." Gathering Damien back in his arms, he reached between them and cut along the crook of his own neck with a knife, then cradled his friend's head to his throat. "Drink," he urged. He could sense Damien's hesitation at first, but the vampire finally latched onto the open wound. "Now, this is going to hurt something fierce, but you have to keep drinking." He knew he had to do this slowly. He had to give Damien's heart time to heal as he pulled the arrow out. Fisting his hand a few times to try to steady the shaking, Larken then took a firm grip on the arrow and pulled it up a bit.

"Ahh!" Larken cried out in pain as Damien's teeth sank deeper into his throat. He knew that the harder bite was just a reaction to the man's own pain, but it still hurt like hell. After a moment, when Damien's clamp eased, he pulled on the arrow a bit more then cried out again as his friend's teeth sank painfully deeper. It felt like hours had passed before the arrow was finally freed. Larken's head spun, as did the world around him. The others had since gathered around them, and being surrounded so closely made the world tilt even more. "Back up," he breathed out as he slumped over, Damien sliding out of his hold to lie in the snow.

"Larken?" Damien's hand came up, and Larken took it in his own.

"Yes, I'm here. Hang in there, buddy."

His friend's eyes widened and he began to tremble. "Larken!"

Worry had him sitting up straight and clutching onto Damien's hand. "I'm here. I'm here."

"Larken!" Damien's free hand flailed about and Larken caught it and brought it to his chest.

"What, Damien? What? I'm here."

"Oh gods." Damien's voice shook. "I can't see you, Larken. I can't see you!"

"Shh." He caressed his friend's cheek again. "Calm down. You need to take it easy."

"It's poisoned," Remus said from behind him.

Looking over his shoulder, he watched as Remus brought the arrowhead to his nose and sniffed it.

Nodding, Remus said again, "Yes, definitely poison."

Larken's stomach fell. He had to get Damien back to the coven immediately. He may have given his friend a lot of blood, but Damien would need more if they wanted to flush the poison from his bloodstream. He only hoped that there was enough time.

"Get my horse!" he hollered. Once on his mare, he held Damien tightly and kicked his heels into the horse's sides, urging her to go as fast as she could. The half hour race back to the coven went by at what felt like a snail's pace. The longer he rode, the limper Damien became in his arms.

He and the others finally reached the coven and he rushed his friend inside before quickly handing him over to the few vampires that had joined the coven to help the injured.

Larken's hands shook as he watched Damien being taken to the infirmary. There was nothing more he could do. He could only hope that what he had done was enough.

A growl behind him had the hairs on the back of his neck standing on end, and when he turned around, he saw the fire blazing in his sire's eyes. The man's chest heaved and his hands were fisted at his sides.

"Where is he?" Keddrick asked, venom dripping from his words.

Remus looked at him in confusion. "Who?"

Keddrick spun around and headed for the stairs. "Nikolai," he ground out.

* * * *

Standing next to the hearth in the war room, Nikolai stared into the fire, hoping that its dancing flames would take away the horrid visions of Damien being carried into the coven. He'd heard the commotion of men as they had neared the castle and had just reached the bottom of the stairs as Damien had been brought in. His body had been so lifeless, and that scared Nikolai nearly to death. Having heard the others talk of rushing Damien to the medical ward to help him had sent a wave of relief through him. It meant that Damien was still alive—but he didn't know for how long, so he did not follow them. He couldn't. He couldn't watch him die. Seeing Damien being carried away was too much as it was. He couldn't stand by and watch the light fade from his eyes.

And so he'd fled—needing to be alone to pray.

Pinching the bridge of his nose, he swallowed down the sorrow that filled him. If Damien didn't make it, he didn't know what he'd do. He had tried not to think about it, but it was clear that the vampire meant something to him—something *more* than he'd originally thought. His heart ached with the possibility of losing him.

Nikolai jumped as the door swung open, violently slamming into the wall. He stepped back as Keddrick stormed over to him.

Standing before him, Keddrick demanded, "Give me your hands."

Nikolai's heart pounded in his chest—this was an anger he'd never seen before in Keddrick. "What?"

"Give me your fucking hands!"

Stunned, Nikolai obligingly lifted his hands toward the sire. Keddrick grabbed them then wiped his wet and sticky fingers over Nikolai's.

Lifting up Nikolai's hands for him to see, Keddrick spat out, "There, are you happy?" His grip tightened around Nikolai's wrists. "Their blood is now on your hands. *Damien's* blood is now on your hands."

Nikolai stared in horror at the red smeared across his skin. "W-what?"

Keddrick shoved him away, causing him to slam into the hearth.

"Keddrick!" Remus gasped out.

"No." The sire raised his hand to ward off any further protest from the commander. He pointed at Nikolai. "All of this is your fault. You've had every opportunity to prevent this, yet you've done *nothing!*"

With his hackles rising, Nikolai clenched his teeth together. He knew where Keddrick was going with this and it pissed him off. The man had sworn to him that he would never speak of it. "You gave me your word," he ground out.

"Fuck my word!" Keddrick shouted. "My people are dying!" He closed what distance was between them and grabbed Nikolai by the front of his shirt. "They are your people—*your* people are dying. You are the TorDrega. You have a responsibility!" He shoved Nikolai back again.

"The Drágun King?" Khale's question was quiet, but everyone turned to him.

Nikolai trembled as he slowly stepped away from the hearth.

Larken cocked his head to the side as he eyed Khale. "How do you know of the Drágun King?"

Khale's gaze never left Nikolai. "My nursemaid use to tell me stories of a time of peace under the ruling of the Drágun King... A time of the TorDrega." His brow furrowed as he eyed Nikolai closer. "But it can't be. They were just stories."

Keddrick shook his head. "I promise you, they are very real." He looked back to Nikolai. "It is your time to rise. It's your time to claim what is yours, Nikolai."

Feeling the acid rising up the back of his throat, Nikolai swallowed down the vile liquid. His gaze shot over to his brother who stood there, his eyes wide and a stricken look across his features. He'd never meant for Bo to find out this way. A knot formed in his throat and he shook his head. He couldn't do this. "I've spent my whole life protecting my brother, and now you've compromised his safety."

Keddrick threw his hands in the air. "Oh, for the gods' sake! Your brother is plenty protected. If you haven't noticed, he's got the backing of an entire fucking coven, not to mention one dangerously protective mate." His stance seemed to relax a little.

"He will be fine. And if there's anybody out there that needs you to accept your fate, it's Bo. You want to protect him? Then claim what is rightfully yours. Pavarus is yours to rule. *Now fight for it.*"

Nikolai shook his head. "I can't."

Keddrick glared at him. "You can't? That's it? So saving your people is pointless? I guess that includes Damien then, yes? You have no desire to save him? Well, the poor man is fighting for his life as we speak." Keddrick turned and headed for the door. "I guess I should just put him out of his misery now and save him the trouble."

Rage surged through Nikolai, his body vibrating as the urge to kill filled him. "You will not!" The booming of his voice echoed throughout the room, causing Keddrick to pause.

When Keddrick turned back to face Nikolai, his eyes widened.

Nikolai's lip pulled back in a snarl as he ground his teeth together, his now lengthened fangs painfully embedded into his bottom lip. When Keddrick's eyebrows pulled together and his eyes narrowed, Nikolai realized that he'd shifted to his *true* form. The coolness behind his glare told him that his eyes had changed and the silver irises now glowed. Glancing down to his hands, he looked at his longer and sharper fingernails, and the light gray skin beneath the blood smears. Closing his eyes, he shifted a little, stretching out the wings that had emerged from his back. He hadn't even registered the sound of his shirt ripping to free them.

It had been over a century since he'd been in this form, and he was beyond mortified that he'd revealed himself this way.

Opening his eyes, he watched as his skin faded to a cream color, like it had been before. The velvety touch of his wings brushed against the bare skin of his back through the rips of his shirt as he tucked them in behind him, but all he really wanted to do was wrap them around himself like a cocoon and hide from the others. Nikolai looked to Bo again—this wasn't how his brother should've found out. The way he'd shared their family history with Bo before had been unfair. This was worse. He opened his mouth to apologize, but words failed him. Tears pricked at his eyes as Bo crossed the room toward him. He looked down into a loving amber gaze and his resolve melted. All he'd ever wanted was to protect Bo.

His brother glanced around to the others. "May we have the room, please?"

A moment of silence passed then Keddrick gave a short nod and motioned for everyone to leave.

Once the door was closed, Bo looked back up at him. "Over the past weeks I've had time to think about everything you told me before, and I must say..."

This was it. This was where Bo would tell him how hurt and angered he was at Nikolai for keeping such secrets—so many lies.

Bo reached up and cupped the side of his face. "I'm so proud of you."

His breath caught and his tears began to fall.

Bo smiled and wiped them away. "You are the strongest person I know. While I am more than surprised at this new revelation, I will say that if you have the ability to save so many lives—more than my own—then I agree with Keddrick. You need to do what is right. This world is being torn apart at the hands of Gravaick." He looked deep into Nikolai's eyes. "Do you have the ability to stop that?"

Nikolai wasn't sure. He knew he was powerful, but he'd never tested that power, too afraid that someone would see it, would somehow find out about him. At least that's what he'd told himself. Second-guessing everything he did was what kept them safe.

Bo took his face into both of his hands then. "Tell me, brother. Can you stop him?"

Trembling, Nikolai accepted what he'd always truly known. "Yes," he breathed out.

A beautiful smile blessed him in return. Bo stood on his tiptoes and wrapped his arms around his shoulders, hugging him close. "I believe in you," he whispered.

Nikolai embraced him in return. "I've tried to be so strong for you."

Bo tightened his hold. "I know, and I love you for that." Releasing him, his brother then glanced around to Nikolai's back. Looking back at him, one of Bo's eyebrows arched. "Black wings, eh?" Bo's features settled. "And without turning into a Drágun? Wow, I never saw that one coming."

Nikolai let out an exhausted chuckle. "Yeah, I'm just full of surprises."

Bo smirked. "I can see that," he said as he motioned to Nikolai's fangs. "What else can you do?"

It took little concentration for Nikolai to pull his wings into his back again, and he hissed as his skin molded back together — the same burning sensation just like when his skin had torn apart to release them. Then after retracting his fangs he replied, "Not much else other than that."

* * * *

Larken quickened his steps down the hall to Khale's quarters. Once they'd left the war room, Khale had seemed like he was in a hurry and had walked off while Larken had been having a word with Keddrick. Finding out that Nikolai was the Drágun King was unreal. He'd had a feeling that Nikolai was keeping something from them, but he'd never suspected it'd be anything like that.

Keddrick telling them that the Drágun King ruled all of Pavarus had his mind whirling. Did this mean that was what Nikolai was going to do? Would Larken then have to serve him instead of Keddrick? He wasn't too keen on that idea, but ultimately he'd do whatever it took to keep his people safe.

He wondered, though, if Nikolai would live up to the fantasy tale of greatness that the—*what had Keddrick called it?*—TorDrega was made out to be. Was Nikolai really that strong and powerful?

Coming up to Khale's room, Larken found the door open. Stepping inside, he spotted Khale hustling around his room, gathering things and placing them in a bag.

Larken stepped closer to him. "What are you doing?"

Gasping, Khale spun around. "Shit, Larken, don't sneak up on me like that." Grumbling, he went about packing his bag again.

"I asked you a question."

"I have to go," Khale said over his shoulder.

"Where?"

"Home. Finding out that another Drágun King exists after so long is big. It's something my father would definitely want to know."

Larken frowned and put his hand on Khale's shoulders, urging the vampire to look at him. "The sun set hours ago. You'll never make it before the sun rises again."

Shaking his head, Khale pulled away from his touch. "If I hurry, I can make it to Havenbort before daybreak. There are humans there that transport vampires during the daytime, so I'll do that."

"No." It was a simple statement, and Larken couldn't have been clearer with it.

Slowly turning to look at him, Khale asked, "Excuse me?"

"I said no. You won't be telling your father anything about this."

"I beg your pardon, but again, this is big news. If I don't tell him, there'll be hell for me to pay when he finds out."

Did the man really not see it? And here Larken thought that Khale was with them to help protect their people. "If you tell your father, then word of the TorDrega will spread like a wildfire."

"So?"

He sighed. "Don't you get it? We've just found out that we've got a great weapon to use against Gravaick and if that asshole finds out what Nikolai is then our one chance at the upper hand is gone. This needs to remain within these walls."

Shaking his head, Khale said, "There were others in that room that heard the same thing I did. Who's to say they won't run their mouths off."

"All the men in that room already knew that Nikolai was different. Granted we didn't know he was *that* different, but we still knew he's a descendant of the Airos clan. And I know my men. They are thinking the same thing I am, that this needs to stay quiet."

Khale's face pinched in distress. "But, Larken, I have to—"

"No," he stated again. He couldn't let their advantage be compromised. "As your Second Commander, I am ordering you to stay here."

Khale's expression turned to one of shock, then annoyance.

"I hope you'll come to understand my reason."

Glaring up at him, Khale gritted out, "Yes, sir."

The look on the vampire's face told Larken that he'd pushed the wrong button, but it had to be done. With nothing more to say, he left.

He had a feeling that the man was going to hold that one against him for quite some time. While Larken had been Khale's superior the entire time the man had been there, he'd never really acted like it with him, and it almost bothered him to do it now. But he had to do what was right for his people, regardless of his feelings for Khale.

Chapter Twelve

Wallace stood stock-still as Gravaick stared angrily at Flagos. The evening had started on a troubling note, and he feared that it would end that way as well. The attack on the vampires had been foolish but, as much as he hated to think in such a way, he was happy to see that some of the Dráguns had been taken down too. The fewer men Gravaick had on his side, the better chance he, Sove and the others had at parting from Gravaick's rule.

With his eyes shining red, Gravaick tilted his head to the side as he scowled at Flagos. "So, you went against my orders?"

Flagos gave a short nod. "Yes, my lord."

"After I specifically told you not to?"

"Yes, my lord."

Crossing his arms over his chest, Gravaick ground out, "You idiot. What the fuck were you thinking? You knew you were outnumbered!"

Something seemed to spark inside Flagos and the man straightened his stance. "I had the opportunity to end it all—to take Keddrick down. How could I—?"

The Drágun's words were cut off as Gravaick grabbed him by the throat. "Yet you missed! You failed! Then you still continued to lead my men into a pointless battle." Seeming disgusted, Gravaick released him and began to pace.

Breathing heavily, Flagos rubbed his throat. "That is why I had everyone retreat almost immediately. Very few were lost."

"How many?"

Wallace held his breath when Flagos' gaze turned to Sove. He knew that this was coming. He knew that going against Flagos had been a bad idea. But he also agreed with his friend. It had been a dangerous decision to make, but they had to start their resistance somewhere.

"Six men were lost, my lord."

Gravaick's eyes narrowed. "It should have been seven."

Wallace could see the worry in Flagos' features. "It might have been less had I the full support like I ordered."

You bastard. This was it, the wrath of their ruler was now turned toward them. Leaning to the side a bit, Wallace brushed the backs of his fingers against Sove's — it was the only way he knew how to show his friend that he was there for him. His body went rigid as Gravaick slowly walked toward them.

"Explain yourselves," Gravaick ordered as he glared at the eight of them.

"I'm the one who made the decision not to fight," Sove answered. Gravaick stopped before him and Sove visibly tensed.

"And why is that?" Gravaick growled.

"I only wanted to do as you commanded, and I knew the others would feel the same. We live to serve you, my lord, not him." Sove bowed his head. "Please do not blame the others. I ordered them to stand down."

Wallace's heart thundered in his chest. He wanted to take the blame as well, he had helped talk to the others, but he did as Sove had wanted and remained quiet.

"So, in following my commands, you disobeyed Flagos' orders?" Gravaick asked. When Sove nodded, he continued, "You let your fellow Dráguns be slaughtered. Six of them gone now."

"I'm sorry, my lord. Please forgive me."

Gravaick's expression hardened right before he pulled his dagger from its sheath and buried it in Sove's chest.

It took everything Wallace had not to move, not to shout out and help his friend. Instead, he just watched as Sove slowly sank to the ground. *He would want me to stay strong.*

"Well, look at that," Gravaick said amusingly. "I guess it was seven."

Flagos chuckled, but his humor died quickly as Gravaick's livid glare pierced him.

"You think that settles the score? That all is forgiven?" Walking across the cave to an assortment of weapons, Gravaick picked up a whip. Going back over to Flagos, he nodded his head in the direction of the entrance. "Outside," he spat. "Now."

Wallace shook with disgust at the excitement that filled the room. Seeing the other Dráguns happy to be witnessing a lashing was disturbing.

Stalo and a few others hesitated to follow, but Wallace shook his head and mouthed 'go'. He wanted to stay behind for Sove, but if too many stayed, it would catch Gravaick's attention.

As soon as the cave was empty, he dropped to his knees and gathered his friend in his arms. "Sove," he croaked out. Blood poured from the man's chest as he gasped for air, and Wallace wiped it away as best he could. "Hang on. You're going to be fine."

Sove shook his head. When he reached up, Wallace took his hand. "Don't—" his friend rasped, then he coughed and blood began to trickle out of the corner of his mouth. "Don't stop."

Remorse gripped at Wallace's chest and he held Sove's hand tighter.

His mouth opening and closing several times, Sove finally whispered, "Save them." Then, on an exhale, he stilled.

Wallace clenched his teeth together as he tried not to scream in anger. Bringing his friend closer, he buried his face in the crook of Sove's neck and whispered, "I will. I promise."

* * * *

When Khale hadn't joined them for breakfast the next evening, and Larken hadn't seen him in the few hours following, he went looking for him. When he reached Khale's room and noticed that his things were gone, Larken's heart pounded with fear.

Racing down to the training room, he found Ile and pulled the man aside. "Have you seen Khale? Do you know where he is?" Larken asked hurriedly.

Ile sneered at him a bit, showing his obvious dislike of Larken. "Yes."

"And?"

"And what?"

"Where is he?" Larken all but shouted. His outburst caught many of the others' attention and he noticed Remus heading his way.

"What's going on?" Remus asked as he neared.

Larken ignored him and kept his focus on Ile. "So where is he?"

Ile's features tightened, but he finally answered, "He went home. I don't know why, so don't bother even asking."

Larken didn't need to ask. While rushing toward the warm room in search of his sire, he ended up running into Keddrick and Nikolai in the entrance hall. "Sire, I have to go."

Keddrick looked at him questioningly. "Where?"

"To Allengard."

Remus then entered the room and stood next to him. "What is going on?"

Larken knew he didn't have time to tell them everything, so he summed it up. "Khale went back home to tell his father about Nikolai." Thankfully, the looks on their faces told him he didn't have to further explain himself. "Please, I must go now."

Shaking his head, Remus said, "Now? You can't go now. We're too many hours into the night and you'll never make it there before daybreak, no matter how fast your mare is."

Larken already had an answer for that. "I can run faster than my horse."

Remus' eyes widened. "Are you crazy? It's colder than hell out there. Your feet will freeze from the snow before you even make it to Havenbort."

"Please..." Larken looked back to his sire. "Please, let me go. I have to stop him."

Keddrick crossed his arms over his chest and looked to Nikolai.

After a moment, Nikolai finally nodded and started to untuck his shirt. "All right, you can ride on my back."

Shaking his head, Larken said, "No, I need to do this alone."

"But I can fly faster than you can run."

"I... I don't have time to tell you why, but this is something that I need to do on my own."

"Be reasonable, Larken," Remus said.

"No."

Both he and Remus looked to their sire.

"All right, go."

Larken didn't stick around to hear Remus' protests. He ran upstairs to grab his cloak and put on his thicker boots then was out of the coven and on his way to Allengard.

* * * *

Khale stood patiently, waiting to hear what his father thought of there being another Drágun King.

Vardel stood silent for a while before he finally said, "Very interesting."

That's it? "Father, I—"

Before Khale could say more, his father shouted, "Ellis."

Vardel's personal guard entered the study and bowed. "Yes, sir?"

"I want you to send word to the other chancellors that we must meet tomorrow evening."

"Yes, sir. I'll do that straight away."

"What? Wait, Ellis." Khale looked to Vardel. "Father, I told you. Larken said that this needs to be kept quiet."

Ignoring him, Vardel waved his hand, gesturing for Ellis to leave.

"Father, please—"

"Would this be the same warrior you desecrated yourself with before you left for Sarren?"

"Y-yes, sir," Khale answered, finding it hard to speak past the lump that had quickly formed in his throat.

Narrowing his eyes, Vardel stared at him, seeming to look inside Khale and search out his deepest secrets. "You did it again, didn't you?"

"No."

Vardel backhanded him. "You lie! I can see it in your eyes!"

Khale's palms began to sweat. "Please, Father. I didn't—"

"On your knees," Vardel cut in.

"But, Father—"

"*On your knees!*"

Lowering his head, Khale began to tremble as he slowly sank down to the floor. He wished the strength and sureness he'd felt at the coven at not being under Vardel's command would help him now, but being back in the man's presence had rekindled the cowardliness his father made him feel. There was something about the man that sucked all confidence out of whomever he was around. Khale wanted to stand up to him, but for some reason couldn't.

He cried out when the first hit of his father's cane came down on his back.

* * * *

The sky was starting to lighten, so Larken ground his teeth together and pushed his body harder. He needed to move faster if he wanted to make it to Vardel's in time. He couldn't even feel his feet anymore and his legs were like heavy blocks of ice, but he pushed on anyway. He had just entered Allengard, and his destination was only another mile away.

By the time Vardel's home came into view, Larken's skin was starting to burn. The sun had crested the horizon and was eating at his flesh as he raced to the castle doors. When he found them locked, Larken hollered out and pounded on the large doors. It seemed like forever passed before he heard a man's voice on the other side.

"Who is it?"

"It is Larken, Second Commander of the warrior coven. Let me in!" To his relief he heard the locks turn, and he pushed his way inside the moment the butler opened the door. Stumbling to a halt, Larken wanted to fall to his knees—his body desperately needed to rest—but he knew he couldn't waste time. "Where is your master?" he panted.

"Sir, if you'd please sit down, I'll—"

"Where is he? Where is Khale?"

"Sir, please—"

Larken knew he'd get nowhere with the man, so he shouted, "Khale? Vardel?"

The doors to the study across the entryway swung open. "What is the meaning of this?" Vardel said angrily.

Opening his mouth to ask the man where Khale was, Larken paused when he saw Khale inside the room, his head bowed as he sat in a high-backed chair. He knew right then that it was too late. He returned his gaze to Vardel. "He told you."

It wasn't a question, but Vardel answered anyway. "Yes. And I must say, I'm quite surprised to learn of it—not sure yet that I believe it—but once the rest of the council hears about it, I know we'll come to a conclusion about what to do with Nikolai." Without another word, Vardel walked away, shooting Larken a smug look before he turned a corner.

With Khale in view again, Larken's heart sank as he stared at him, his legs feeling like mush as he slowly walked to the doorway of the study. "How could you do this?" Khale didn't answer him—didn't even look at him—and his heart sank a little more. "I trusted you at your word that you wouldn't come here." Forget that he'd given the vampire a direct order, the betrayal stung more. He was so sure that Khale had felt something for him, but how could the man have then gone behind his back like that?

The more he thought about it, the more his hurt was replaced with anger. "I trusted you," he said again, a little more vehemence in his voice. "When you signed your name in the daya, you swore your loyalty to the coven. But it was a lie! You betrayed us all by coming here." Larken took in a deep breath, trying to calm his nerves. "You betrayed me."

To Larken's amazement, Khale said nothing. The man simply got up, flashed Larken a quick glance, then left through a door on the other side of the room. Now Larken's heart didn't simply hurt—it was broken. Making his way to the staircase, he eased himself down onto the steps. He needed to rest, and as soon as the sun set again he was leaving. When the butler began to walk toward him with a displeased expression, Larken glared at the man, daring the vampire to bother him, to ask him to leave. Seeing that

Larken had no intention of moving, the butler sneered and walked away.

But he wasn't left alone for very long. Not even a half hour later, an old, portly woman strolled right up to Larken and glared down at him. "So, are you just going to sit there all day, boy?"

"That's the plan," he grumbled.

With her hands on her hips, she said in an irritated tone, "Do you have any idea what that young man has been through? What he's going through now?"

Larken gritted his teeth. He knew she was referring to Khale. "I don't really care."

"Of course you do."

Giving her an exasperated look, he asked, "Who are you?"

"My name is Ragi, and I'm Khale's nursemaid. Now, don't change the subject."

Larken was starting to get frustrated with her. "Listen, Ragi, I *don't* care what he's been through. All I care about is what he's done to me... I mean the coven."

Shaking her head, she said, "Boy, if you knew what Khale's been through, then you'd understand why he's done what he did."

"How do you even know what's going on?"

"Because I just talked to him in his room. I'm the closest thing that young man has to a mother. He tells me everything."

"Well, then you can obviously see why *I. Don't. Care.*"

"Don't get cross with me, boy." When Larken started to speak again, she waved a hand at him and said, "Just do one thing for me. Go talk to him."

"He didn't say anything to me before. I'm going to take that as a sign that he doesn't *want* to talk."

"That's because he was hurting. He still is."

Larken swallowed hard and an ache formed in his chest. How could Khale be hurting? Khale was the one who was in the wrong. He had no right to feel hurt.

"Please, go talk to him," Ragi said.

"No."

Tossing her hands in the air, she let out a frustrated huff. "It's not as if you have anything better to do right now."

"But I do – sitting here."

Her expression turned to one of sadness. "Please," she begged. "If you talk to him, you'll understand his reasons. His father..." She glanced away for a second, seeming to gather herself. "You need to know what's happening to him. And when you realize what's going on, I pray that you'll take him away from here."

Larken thought on that for a moment. Ragi obviously loved Khale, so why would she want him to be taken away? But then he thought of her mentioning Vardel, and his stomach sank. "Where is he?"

Her features softened. "He's in his bathroom. Just go down this hall and you'll see another set of stairs – "

Larken didn't wait for her to finish. He already knew the way.

"There's a robe on his bed," she hollered after him. "If you could take it to him, I'd appreciate it."

Chapter Thirteen

Hunched over in the tub, Khale rested his chin against his knees as he swirled the end of his braid around in the bathwater. He couldn't get the look on Larken's face out of his mind. The man hated him now. There was no mistaking that. He'd betrayed Larken and there was nothing he could do to change it. He'd truly thought telling his father would be all right, but he knew now it had been a terrible mistake. He could see that his father had never had the intention to give him anything — love, respect, or even kindness — in return for his help. Just as Khale had betrayed Larken, he'd been betrayed by his father.

He closed his eyes as the ache in his chest grew. He'd just lost everything. Even more so, he'd lost the man he loved. It had taken Larken's rejection to realize how deep his feelings were for the man.

Tilting his head down to rest his forehead against his knees, Khale held back the tears. Crying would get him nowhere right now. It didn't matter how much he hurt. He'd have to deal with it. He was on his own now and needed to start thinking about where he was going to go and what he was going to do.

When he heard footsteps behind him, he took a deep breath to compose himself. Standing up, he said, "It's about time, Ragi, the water's freezing. Was my robe hiding or…?" Khale's words died off as he turned around and saw Larken. The scowl on the vampire's face had his heart racing. "Larken. What…? What are you doing here?" He spotted his robe in Larken's hand and got out of the tub to take it.

While Khale donned the plush material, Larken asked, "What were those?"

Swallowing hard, Khale tightened the sash around his waist. "What's what?" he asked as he passed by Larken and hurried into his bedroom. He headed straight to his wardrobe, refusing to meet Larken's stare.

A growl sounded behind him. "Don't play with me. I asked you a question."

Khale's nerves grated. "Stop ordering me around, damn it."

"I asked you a simple question, so answer it."

Khale roughly sifted through his clothes till he found the shirt and pants he was looking for. Since Larken had now seen his back, he didn't try to hide it as he disrobed then got dressed. When he turned around, Larken was glaring at him. "Things are never simple when it comes to you, Larken. So what makes you think your question is any different?"

Larken's brow pulled down in a frown. "Me? What the fuck does my question have to do with me?"

Tightening his jaw, Khale contemplated his next words. He hadn't meant to say that to him, and he really didn't want to tell Larken why he'd gotten his beating. "It doesn't matter." Shaking his head, he asked, "What are you doing here anyway? Where's Ragi?"

Larken stormed across the room and came to a stop inches away from him. "Do not ignore me, Khale. Answer my fucking question."

Khale's heart raced at the heat in Larken's eyes. He remembered when that heat was from their passion, from their time together — time he'd never get again. "Please, Larken, just forget it," he replied softly.

His features softening, Larken regarded him. "Your back is a mess of bruises and lesions. You can't tell me to just forget that. How did it happen? Was it from the other night, from the fight?" Larken shook his head. "No, I already saw those marks fading away, and they're too fresh," he mumbled to himself. "Khale, that had to have happened today. Now tell me what —"

"I deserved it, all right!" Khale interrupted. "I went against his orders, so I got what was coming to me." He couldn't believe he'd just said that. He knew he didn't deserve it, but he had nothing else. He closed his eyes and bowed his head. "Please, Larken, just leave it be."

A warm hand cupped his cheek, and Khale looked up at Larken in surprise. He saw worry in the vampire's eyes, and his chest tightened. He leaned into the touch, savoring what was probably the last one he'd get.

"Your father did this to you?" Larken asked gently. "Whatever the reason, he had no right to do it."

Khale sighed. "What does it matter, now? It's done and over with."

Larken's hand dropped. "What does it matter? Are you serious? The man beats you and you don't care?"

Khale's gaze shot up and he pierced Larken with a glare. "Of course I care!" He shoved Larken back and walked across the room. "You have no idea what's going on, so you have no right to say that I don't care."

"Then tell me!" Larken yelled back.

Spinning around to face him, Khale snapped out, "All I've ever wanted was one thing from that man" — he threw his hand up—"and I'll never get it. I had it not once, but twice within my grasp and I ruined them both at the same time."

"What do you want, Khale?"

Looking away, he shook his head. Larken would think he was weak for wanting it.

"I won't think that," Larken said softly.

Khale stared up at him in shock. Had he said that out loud?

Larken crossed the room and took Khale's face within his hands once again. "Please, tell me."

Begging his bottom lip not to tremble, Khale whispered, "Love." He sucked in a shuddering breath. "All I've ever wanted was to be loved."

Sadness filled Larken's gaze. "That doesn't make you weak. If anything, it makes you stronger. It's all right to want that. Everyone deserves to be loved."

"Yet I haven't. I've spent my entire life trying to earn my father's love. I suffered through the beatings and emotional torture, all in the hopes of getting the smallest amount of emotion from that man, but I know now that I'll never get it." He jerked out of Larken's hold. "I don't think I'll ever know what it feels like to be loved." A lump formed in his throat and he had to look away.

"The love of a father, is that the only love you want?"

Khale squeezed his eyes shut as they started to sting, and shook his head.

"You want to be in love?" Larken asked quietly.

Khale nodded, still not looking at him.

"You said you had love not once, but twice within your grasp. Am I that other love?"

With his body trembling and heart bared, ready to be cut down by this man, Khale took the leap and nodded again.

"Well, then you have it."

Spinning around, he met Larken's gaze. "What?"

This time, Larken's hands shook as he brought them up to cup Khale's face. "I said you have it."

He searched Larken's gaze for the truth in his words, and the light he found within clear blue eyes said it all. His heart flooded with warmth. All of the years he'd gone without, and here it was within his grasp. He wanted it. He needed it. It had to be true. After everything they'd suffered together, he loved this man, and he needed love in return. Was Larken actually giving him what he longed for?

Larken leaned in, their lips mere inches apart, and whispered, "You have it, my love."

Khale's knees threatened to give out as Larken placed his mouth over his. He felt it. He knew it all within that single kiss.

Larken wound his arms around Khale and pulled him close. Of all the times they'd been together, this felt different. A warmth spread throughout him as Larken stole his breath away, tenderness and passion molding them together.

Larken broke the kiss and buried his face in the curve of Khale's neck. "I love you, Khale, but I'm not sure how to do this anymore." His words sounded so tired and pained—like a man who'd given up.

Khale threaded his fingers through Larken's hair. "There is nothing you have to *do*," he breathed out. "You just have to feel."

Larken's mouth was suddenly against his again and Khale reveled in it. The taste, the touch, the emotion that flowed with every movement. Larken sought out his tongue and he gladly opened up for him. They let their passion loose as their tongues tangled and lips pressed together.

They slowly made their way to his bed. Larken laid his body over Khale's, and Khale waited for the vampire to give him his instructions as always — don't move. It was a power play that Khale could tell Larken very much enjoyed, and he happily obliged, but he desperately craved to be able to touch the man in return.

He waited as Larken undressed him, the man's mouth traveling along his skin as it was uncovered. He waited as Larken quickly rid himself of his own attire. The vampire then settled between his legs and trailed kisses along his jaw. His fingers itched to explore, and the sound of his name on Larken's lips was the permission he'd been dying for.

Wrapping his arms and legs around Larken, Khale kissed the man with everything he had. He roamed his hands everywhere he could reach as Larken devoured his mouth in return. It was fierce and passionate all the same. This was the connection he craved. The feel of Larken against him was all that he needed.

They took their time. Larken gently prepared him, massaging Khale's inner passage as their lips barely parted. Then their gazes locked as Larken entered him, inch by blissful inch.

They moved together—kissing and touching and cherishing every moment they had. It wasn't hurried this time. It was slow and sweet—they made love.

"You're mine now. Forever and always," Larken whispered in his ear. "I love you."

Khale's chest tightened at Larken's words, a pleasant ache taking hold of his heart. "I love you too."

"Tell me you want me as your mate."

"*Yes.*" It was all Khale could say. He was too overwhelmed with joy to express how much he wanted Larken.

When Larken's fangs sank into the curve of his neck, Khale immediately felt the bond between them spread throughout his body. Biting Larken in return, he finished the bond, claiming Larken as his mate. Khale's breath caught as a slight sting flared on his chest. Looking down, he watched as Larken's family mark appeared on his right pec.

"So beautiful," Larken said as he ran his fingers over Khale's chest.

Looking up, Khale watched as his mark appeared on Larken. Knowing that they were mates made him happier than he'd ever been before. He felt complete. He had a family now with not only Larken, but Larken's brothers at the coven too. Khale finally felt loved. And seeing the love in Larken's eyes pushed him over the edge and he came, Larken's shuddering release following soon after.

* * * *

Slowly opening his eyes, Khale smiled as he felt the warmth of Larken's body against his. His mind wandered back, reliving the pleasurable hours that had passed. They'd spent the rest of the day and halfway into the next night making love. It had been the best time of his life, and one he intended to repeat in the future.

Khale was fantasizing about one particular memory of him pressed against the wall, Larken buried deep inside him, when his stomach growled. It was then that he realized he hadn't eaten since the evening he'd left the coven, and he was sure that Larken would be just as famished as he. While reluctant to leave his mate, Khale slipped out of bed and got dressed, and with one last look at Larken, he headed down to the kitchen.

The hustle and bustle that commenced when he arrived was pleasantly appealing. There was something about the sounds and smells that grounded him. This was life. This was normal. The servants were here for one thing, to take care of the people that resided within the household. And, as strange as it was, it was an act he wanted to perform for Larken. He wanted to take care of him—even if it meant just bringing the man dinner.

He playfully dodged the cook's swatting hand a few times as he picked from her smorgasbord. He gathered meats, cheeses and a couple of bowls of stew. She successfully made contact with the back of his hand as he reached out to steal a loaf of bread.

"Aye, woman, can a man not eat?"

She glared at him, but the hint of a smirk belied her actions as she pointed at him. "Now don't you be stealing from my table, boy. You'll just have to wait and eat dinner with the rest of them."

Khale couldn't hold back his smile. "But I'm not eating dinner with everyone else. I'm dining in my room tonight."

Her eyes narrowed, but soon glittered with happiness as she surveyed his plate, no doubt realizing that there was enough food for two. Still, she snatched back the bread he held in his hand. "I'll not have you taking this, though." Her smirk spread into a lovely grin. "Here." She handed him another loaf, one that was still warm. "This one's a bit fresher." Seriousness filled her expression as she reached out and gently squeezed his arm. "It's good to see you smile, Master Khale."

He wasn't sure how he'd missed it before, but seeing the look on her face made him realize that he wasn't as alone as he'd always thought. Most of the servants in the household had been with him almost all his life, but he'd been too busy trying to gain an ounce of feeling from his father that he'd missed how much the people around him meant to him. Having Larken's love was everything to him, but he was glad to realize that there were others out there, and he was determined to let them know how much they meant to him as well—starting with Ragi.

But that would have to wait. Right now he had a man to feed. Feeling ridiculously happy, Khale was light on his feet as he headed back to his room. His mind was once again lost in the previous hours' activities when he was suddenly slammed against the wall, pain coursing through his head when it made contact with the hard stone.

Dazed, he struggled as best he could as two guards grabbed his arms. He opened his mouth to yell at them, but his words were lost when he felt a pinch at his neck. He stared in confusion at Ellis as the vampire backed away, a sewing needle in his hand. Warmth spread over Khale's skin as his mind began to spin.

"It's beautiful, isn't it?"

Khale stiffened at the sound of his father's voice. He watched in fear and hurt as the man came forward, an Athis Dey held delicately between his fingers.

A malicious grin spread over his father's face. "I personally think it's quite stunning."

Khale began to shake. "You... You poisoned me?"

Vardel's grin slipped away. "Don't worry, it wasn't enough to kill you—just weaken you."

Khale's fear faded, but his hurt settled deeper. "Why?"

Scowling, Vardel crowded him against the wall. "Because you have disgraced me for the last time." Stepping back, pure hatred in his eyes, he ordered, "Take him away."

Khale hollered and fought back as best he could, but the poison was too strong. His feet dragged along the ground as he was taken to the upper levels. He had a feeling he knew where he was going, but the stark reality of it didn't set in until he saw the narrow staircase that led to the roof. "No. Please, *no*. Larken!"

* * * *

Gasping, Larken shot up in bed, sweat dripping from his brow. He clutched at his chest as he tried to get his bearings. It took a moment to remember where he was, but when he did he immediately began to calm. Getting out of bed, he slowly began to dress. "Khale?" While tying the leather cords of his pants together, he poked his head into the sitting area. "Khale?"

He knew he shouldn't be bothered by the fact that his mate wasn't there—it was the man's house after all—but something didn't feel right. Maybe it was only the lingering adrenaline from his nightmare that had a knot forming in his gut, but whatever it was, he knew he'd only feel better once he'd found Khale. After slipping his boots on, he exited the quarters and began his search. Everyone he stopped and questioned said they hadn't seen him, but how could that be? There were only so many places a man could hide, even in a house this big—someone was bound to have seen him.

In the end, as much as he didn't want to, he went to Vardel. He found the chancellor in his study, relaxing in a high-backed chair by the hearth.

"Bursting into a person's private quarters without knocking is quite rude," Vardel snarled.

"Yes, well, my pleasantries have run dry. My apologies," he said sarcastically as he gave a mock bow. "I'll be happy to get out of your hair once you tell me where Khale is."

The chancellor's scowl faded into a satisfied grin, a grin that Larken didn't like one bit. It was then that Larken noticed what the man was holding. He knew what it was right away, and the flower was just as he had imagined it would look like. "What did you do to him?" he demanded.

"What I should have done years ago."

Rage surged through him as he yanked Vardel from his chair by the lapels of his waistcoat. "Where is he?" The chancellor's chuckles fueled his rage and he slammed the man down onto a nearby table. "Answer me!"

Vardel's chuckles deepened as he looked past Larken's shoulder to the ceiling. "The sun is rising." He met Larken's gaze. "You're too late."

No!

Releasing Vardel, Larken ran as fast as he could, his heart pounding in his chest as he raced to the stairs.

He knew what Vardel had done. He'd heard of the council using the method numerous times for executions. To know that Khale was facing that now threatened to suck all the hope out of him. But he couldn't let that slow him down. He had to try. Even if that meant he'd be following Khale to the *other side*. He grabbed the first servant he came across. "The roof! How do I get to the roof!"

* * * *

Khale shook as he stood out in the cold. They had stripped him of all but his pants, and now the bite of winter was eating away at him. But soon it wouldn't matter. Soon he would never feel cold again.

He looked out over the city, looked at the sky as it slowly began to lighten. The sun was minutes away from rising and he could already feel its heat. Khale lowered his head as his mind went to Larken. He hoped that his mate was lying in bed, dreaming peacefully and without a care in the world. It still amazed him to know that Larken loved him, and he hoped his death wouldn't weigh too heavily on the man. Larken deserved the world—Khale only wished it was he who could have given it to him.

A breeze picked up, but a chill failed to pass through him, for the sun's rays crested the horizon and its heat bore into him. Hissing, he crouched down on the rooftop and hugged himself tightly. Tears stung his eyes as he thought of Larken again.

The sound of the roof door bursting open had Khale jumping to his feet. Shocked, Khale watched as Larken cringed and shielded his eyes from the light.

"Khale!" Larken rushed to his side then enveloped him within his arms. "Oh gods, I thought you were already dead." He hugged Khale closely then pulled back to look at him. When Larken's eyes widened at seeing the collar around Khale's neck that was fastened to the roof by a chain, Khale's heart sank. There was no getting out of this, and he had one chance to say goodbye.

Wrapping his arms around Larken, Khale kissed him deeply. "I love you," he whispered against Larken's lips. A slice of pain shot through him as the sky lightened even more, and both of them grunted from the uncomfortable feeling. "You have to go." He pushed Larken away, but the man held steady and stared at him in surprise.

"What? I'm not going anywhere without you. Now come on and help me get this off."

Khale stood still as Larken pulled at the collar. It was no use and he knew it. "Larken, please, don't. You have to go inside. *Now*."

"No." Larken yanked harder, causing the metal to dig into Khale's neck.

Crying out, Khale grabbed Larken's hands to still him. "Stop, please. It's no use."

"I said I'm not leaving you. Now help me."

Tears gathered in Khale's eyes again as he watched Larken begin to pull at the chain linked to his collar. He knew the chain would never give. He'd already tried pulling at it relentlessly once the poison of the Athis Dey had worn off, giving him his strength back. "Larken—"

"Help me!" Larken pulled harder, his knuckles turning white against the metal.

Sadness filled him as he reached out and cupped Larken's face. His mate's struggles ceased as Khale urged him to look at him. "It's enchanted. It'll never give. Now please, you can save yourself. *Go inside*," he pleaded. He shuddered as the light of the sun trickled higher over the city's homes and a painful ache slowly formed beneath his skin.

Larken panted from his efforts and looked to him with sorrow in his eyes. Shaking his head, he took hold of Khale's face and pressed their lips together. "How can I leave you? How can you ask me that?"

Khale hugged him closely and buried his face into the crook of Larken's neck. He took a deep breath, savoring the scent of his mate, then pulled back. His bottom lip trembled as he looked at Larken's reddening face. "Please, for me, go inside."

Larken stared at him, then he glanced to the eastern horizon. Khale saw the emotion flooding the man's gaze when he looked back to him. Wrapping his arms around Khale again, Larken hugged him tightly.

The heat of his tears warmed Khale's burning cheeks as he embraced his mate in return. This was it. This was goodbye, and his heart bellowed in pain. He gasped, though, when Larken suddenly turned them so his back was to the rising sun, blocking Khale as much as he could. Khale still knew there was no way he'd survive, but the act itself had tears gushing out of him. He sobbed and pressed harder into Larken's hold.

"I love you," Larken breathed out as he rested his cheek on top of Khale's head.

Khale trembled as he replied, "And I love you." He wept silently as the sun's rays started to burn his arms. When Larken began to shudder violently, Khale sobbed out his mate's name, and in return Larken held him tighter. The air around them hummed loudly, the sounds of their cries ringing in his ears, and Khale prayed that it'd be over quickly.

The sound of a woman shouting his name had him looking over his shoulder. He spotted Ragi in the doorway, her arm raised as she threw something at him. He caught the tiny object then stared down in disbelief at the key he held. He had no time to process the moment in his head when Larken snatched the key from him. Fumbling a bit, Larken managed to unlock his collar and they raced to the door. Once inside, Ragi slammed the door closed then leaned back against it, panting as she wiped at her brow.

Khale was engulfed within Larken's arms again, and they held onto each other. "Oh gods," Khale gasped out. He had thought that they were surely going to die and the relief that they were safe overwhelmed him.

Pulling back, Larken then looked him over. "Are you all right?"

Nodding, Khale gave him a weak smile. Larken briefly returned it before he kissed Khale. It was love and joy and fear that they'd almost lost each other that filled the kiss, and Khale never wanted it to end. But it did when Larken went rigid in his arms. Stepping back, Larken took one last look at him, pure fury shining in his eyes, then he turned and ran down the stairs. Khale knew immediately what Larken was doing, and he raced after him. He finally caught up to him in his father's study just as Larken slammed Vardel against the wall.

When his mate unsheathed his dagger, Khale sprang forward and grabbed his arm. "Don't!"

Larken looked back at him in confusion. "You dare defend him?"

Khale sighed. "No, but… He's still my father."

"A father that tried to kill you," Larken argued back.

"Yes, I know, but he's also a chancellor, Larken. And if you kill him, you're signing your own death sentence. The council will not stand for him being murdered and they'll see you burned for it."

Releasing a menacing grin, Larken turned back to Vardel. "Then I'll die a happy man."

"Larken!" Khale squeezed the man's arm. "I cannot lose you. Please, don't do this."

Scowling, Larken looked to Vardel and pointed his dagger at him. "He saved your life today. Remember that," he growled, then released him.

Vardel sneered as he pulled at his waistcoat, trying to straighten it. "I would've rather died than be in debt to that man for saving my life."

Khale swallowed down the hurt of his father's words. "Well, fear not. I hold no debt over you. But I do wish to make a deal. In exchange for me not telling the council that you tried to kill me, you must swear that you won't tell them about Nikolai."

Vardel's features tightened as he glared at Khale. "I swear," he finally answered.

While his heart ached, Khale also felt a sense of relief. Not wanting to spend another moment with the man, Khale turned on his heels and exited the room, knowing that Larken was following closely behind.

Out in the hall he spotted Ragi and the grief he felt faded a bit. Going over to her, he gave her a big hug and said, "Thank you." He pulled back and stared at her. "How, though? I knew only one of the guards had the key."

Ragi arched an eyebrow and pursed her lips. "Child, I'll have you know I'm over six hundred years old." She scoffed. "That young pup of a guard stood no chance against me."

Khale couldn't help but smile, then the sound of Larken clearing his throat brought him back to the here and now. They had to get out of there. He didn't want to spend another moment under the same roof as Vardel, especially since it was the one his father had tried to kill him on. "I think I've had just about enough of this place. How about we go home?"

"Agreed," Larken replied.

Larken wrapped an arm around him and they headed for the entrance hall. When he noticed that Ragi wasn't following, he looked back at her. "Well, aren't you coming?" A smile graced her features as she fell into step behind them. There was no way he was leaving her here with Vardel. And besides, he wanted her with him. She was the mother he had never had, and he was going to hold on tightly to her from there on out.

It wasn't long before one of the human servants had the three of them safely secured in a covered cart. Larken held him closely as they swayed with the motion of the uneven road. Guilt began to fill him as he thought of what had gotten him to this point. He was happy to have Larken as his own now, but he wished that it had happened differently. He'd betrayed his love, and it ate away at him that he had done it.

"I'm sorry," he whispered.

Larken looked down at him with a frown. "For what?"

Khale licked his lips and swallowed hard. "For telling my father about Nikolai. Aside from what he promised, I fear it won't be long before word spreads and Gravaick learns of what Nikolai is." He lowered his head in shame. "I'm sorry."

Larken stared at Khale, moved by the sorrow in the man's voice. Larken knew better now. He knew that Khale was truly sorry for what he'd done, and he knew that Khale had been misguided when he'd done it. He wasn't about to hold that against him. Placing his finger under Khale's chin, he urged his mate to look at him. "It's all right. I'm not mad." He smiled to help reassure him. "Besides, I have a feeling something like this wouldn't have gone unnoticed for too long. Gravaick is bound to find out sooner or later. I was just hoping it would be much later."

Khale looked up at him with worry-filled violet eyes. "Really? You're not angry with me? I betrayed—"

Larken silenced him with a kiss. "All I care about right now is the fact that you're safe and in my arms." Khale's warm grin moved him and he leaned down and kissed him again. He knew that the road ahead of them wasn't going to be easy, but as long as they had each other—as long as he had the man he loved—he knew that they'd prevail in the end. They had to, because there was no way he was ever going to lose Khale. Finally coming to terms with what he felt for the vampire had been the best thing that he'd done. He was grateful that he'd moved past his hurt to see what was right in front of him.

About the Author

Hey everyone, I'm Jen and I'm an author of M/M erotic romance. I love M/M romance, both reading and writing it—seriously, what's better than a sexy man... Two sexy men! You can't go wrong there. Though I do dabble in a little bit of M/F romance, my main passion will always be smutting it up with men, men and more men. I try to dedicate as much of my free time to writing as I can—ha! What free time?—but if I'm not typing away on my laptop, you'll find me with my nose buried in a book, or with my loving fiancé debating on what movie to watch and the never-ending back and forth decision of what to have for dinner. I love spending time with my family and fiancé, cuddling with my dog and two cats, and laughing as much as possible—'cause I like to think I'm funny!

Some little tidbits about me are—I love animals of all sorts, I have a really big sweet-tooth, and I've been told I like to talk with my hands (insert hand gestures here).

Jennifer Wright loves to hear from readers. You can find her contact information, website details and author profile page at http://www.totallybound.com.

Totally Bound Publishing